Bitchcraft

Featuring stories by:
S.B. Rhodes
J.A. Cummings
Lindy S. Hudis
Katie Jaarsveld
J.M. Goodrich

Bitchcraft

© 2019 Irish Horse Productions

This is a work of fiction. Names, places, characters, and events are the product of the author's imagination. Any resemblance to any persons, living or dead, is entirely coincidental.

Cover design © 2019 Sassa Brown
Published by Avant Garde Publishing
Edited by Sassa Brown

Table of Contents

Phoenix Rising
By S.B. Rhodes

Phoenix lives a charmed life in a small village with a loyal friend, a loving family, and a budding romance. That is, until she is accused of witchcraft. Is this the end, or will she rise from the ashes like the great Phoenix of legend?

A Charmed Life

Laughter echoed through the air as children ran through fields, playing merrily. A little girl's brown pigtails bounced up and down as she dodged the grasps of her friend who was trying to tag her. A smile spread across her face, nearly ear to ear, her dimples widening as she giggled. A nearby boy climbed a haystack to get a better view of the field as he tried to locate his companions during a game of hide-and-seek.

A toddler played nearby, while his mother picked some flowers. She knelt down and let her young son smell them, then laughed as he opened his mouth in an attempt to eat them. She picked him up and twirled him in the air before pulling him close and giving him a gentle hug. The sun shone brightly behind them, its crepuscular rays cascading over them like a warm halo.

Phoenix sat beneath her favorite tree, taking it all in. She tucked her red hair behind her ear and clutched the book she'd been reading to her chest, preferring to watch the scene before her. The sounds of children laughing provided great comfort to her, for she had come so close to losing everything.

****

The lands were ravaged by fire during the major drought that lasted decades. Crops became scarce, and the villagers feared the worst. Colonies near and far had dwindled in numbers as people died from malnutrition and disease.

Thankfully for them, Phoenix had been born to a powerful family, and she would be their savior. If it had not been for her, the drought likely would have lasted far longer, the damage even more severe, and many more lives lost.

She discovered an old diary that belonged to her grandmother. Unlike the typical trinkets and journals one would expect to find while cleaning out an attic, this particular diary was unique. It was leather-bound and displayed a pentacle on the cover, though at the time, she did not recognize the symbol or its significance.

It wasn't until she showed it to her grandmother that the truth was revealed. "Grandmother, what kind of diary is this?" she asked.

The old woman's face crinkled in delight as a smile spread across her rosy cheeks. Her eyes were filled with a light that Phoenix had not seen in quite some time. "I was hoping the day would come that you would find this book. There is so much that I have been wanting to share with you, but I wanted to wait until the time was right."

"I don't understand," said Phoenix, sitting at the foot of the rocking chair with her hands propped up on her grandmother's leg. "Are there deep, dark secrets in your diary? Did you do something? Were you a bandit? I bet you were mischievous in your younger years, weren't you?"

Grandmother Lorna let out a slight chuckle. "No, nothing like that, though I was quite the scamp; I'll give you that. This, my child, is not an ordinary diary." She rubbed the cover for a moment, seemingly deep in thought. "Many ancient secrets are locked away within its pages. My key is hidden in the vase on my dresser. Will you retrieve it for me, please?"

Phoenix nodded and pulled herself up, careful not to press too hard on the rocking chair as she rose to her feet. She ran to her grandmother's bedroom and peered around the room before entering. As she approached the dresser, she thought she caught a glimpse of movement out of the corner behind her. She looked up at the mirror, then turned around. Nothing was there. *I must be imagining things,* she thought to herself.

She tilted the vase at an angle. The key rattled around in the vase as it made its way to the opening. When it finally dropped onto the desk, Phoenix grabbed it and carefully put the vase back where it belonged. She walked towards the door and shuddered, still feeling as though someone... or something... was in the room with her. She closed the door behind her and returned to the living room, handing her grandmother the key.

"Thank you," she said while unlocking the book. "This was handed down to me by my mother, your great-grandmother Phoenix, after whom you were named."

"You never talk about her very much. What was she like?"

"She was a kind soul, always offering a helping hand to anyone in need. She often took in traveling strangers, filling their bellies and giving them a warm place to sleep before they parted once more. There was no one I admired more."

"She sounds lovely. I can see why Mother would want to honor her, but why Phoenix? That is not a usual name. How did her mother come up with it?"

Grandmother smiled warmly. "That was inspired by the great Phoenix of legend, a bird who rose from the ashes according to ancient mythology."

"That sounds incredible. You have so many interesting stories. How did you learn all this? The only stories anyone tells around here are those you can read for yourself in the Bible."

"I learned them from my mother. She taught me more than any school teacher or pastor ever could… not that they don't try and do the best they can. My mother was just very special and loved learning. She would spend hours reading each day – books of all types and from different areas. Sometimes, she would borrow books from traveling families or listen to tales that originated in their lands."

"And she gave you this book?"

"Oh, yes. This book is very special, and she wanted it to stay in the family, as it always had. It belonged to her mother before her, and her mother's mother before that, and her father before that… for as long as anyone can remember. Many generations have studied and used this book for their craft."

"Craft?" Phoenix asked, confused.

"Yes, dear. Witchcraft."

Phoenix's curiosity was piqued, and she could not wait to hear more. She sat closer and listened attentively as her grandmother told her the stories of their ancestors and the role that witchcraft played in their lives.

"Some people are born with abilities," she explained. "In some cases, they come from powerful witch families like our own. In other cases, the individual is the sole witch in their family, having received a calling from the gods themselves. Perhaps they were witches in a previous life. We do not know, but there is a saying... once a witch, always a witch.

However, it is not enough to merely receive a calling or have certain abilities. Yes, they do make it easier. However, even if you are born a witch, you must dedicate yourself to the craft. Study it, learn all that you can, and practice it. You must continue to develop it, lest it die out altogether. If you forsake your calling, it will forsake you as well."

Phoenix pondered over the information for a while, reading the book from time to time. She had never considered that magick could truly exist in the world. She had been taught that it only existed in fairytales and legends. The real world was far too dark and serious for such fanciful ideas. Her parents certainly did not believe in such things.

Grandmother Lorna had explained that her daughter, Phoenix's mother, had thought herself too mature and logical to believe in magick. Fiona could only bring herself to believe in that which she could see and feel and experience for herself, and magick wasn't it.

"She did have a gift when she was younger," she said, to Phoenix's surprise. "She could understand animals... talk to them, even. She had a special connection with the creatures of the earth, and they all loved her. Unfortunately, as the world began to take notice, they taunted her for her abilities, never really believing what she told them. Over time, they convinced her that it had all been her imagination, and she learned to tune it out."

"How sad," said Phoenix, pulling her knees closer as she sat with her back against the chair. "So, did I have any abilities?"

"I do not know, my child. Your mother did not want me to teach you as I did her. She didn't want your head filled with thoughts of witchcraft, which she considered to be nonsense. So, I could never work with you or help you develop your abilities if they did exist. I often suspected, however, that you might have a connection to the other side."

"Other side?"

"Yes, the spirit realm. From time to time, I would see you suddenly stop what you were doing and turn to face the corner of the room, or you would suddenly become fearful and look as though you saw something nobody else could. Everyone said that it was nothing more than childhood nightmares and imaginary friends, but part of me always wondered."

The lessons continued, and she began to flourish. Material that at first seemed so complex and strange became familiar. Spells that were difficult soon became second nature to her. Eventually, she built up the ability and courage to do something on a larger scale – something that could truly have an impact on others.

She approached her grandmother and asked for assistance, as this was sure to be a difficult task. Besides, she wanted her grandmother to be part of it. Unfortunately, there were no spells or guides to give them aide in her mission, but that did not matter. If there wasn't a spell that could help her, then she would create one.

She studied plant life and herbs, water and its curative properties, and the soil. She learned all that she could until she was ready. They gathered all the materials they needed and met in the barn so as to avoid waking the rest of the family. There, they brewed a potion and bottled it.

Grandmother Lorna looked down, beaming with pride at her young granddaughter. Not only had she taken so well to the lessons and progressed much as a young witch, but she was following her heart and using her power for good. It was what she had always hoped for her. She helped her prepare the cauldron and everything else that she needed for her potion. She was proud to be a part of something so pure and wonderful… to use her power to help others as her own mother did.

As they worked, Phoenix heard a noise coming from outside. She turned and grabbed her grandmother's arm. "What was that?" They started to inch forward, their hearts beating faster. They nearly jumped out of their skins as the family cat walked in and mewed at them. They burst into laughter. "Olive, you silly cat. What are you doing out here?" She pet her for a moment, then returned to her work.

Once they were finished, they took the bottles with them, visiting farms and orchards throughout the night, purifying the land and sprinkling their concoction on the plants. They blessed the lands in each place before moving on to the next.

Once they returned home, Grandmother Lorna hugged Phoenix and told her how much she loved her and how proud she was of her – her beautiful heart, her willingness to use her power for good, and her intellect.

"I always knew you were meant for great things," she said. She then removed the small, preserved carnation from her own dress and carefully pinned it to her granddaughter's.

"But Grandmother, this is so special to you. You wear it always."

"And now, you shall do the same. You are correct. It is special to me, and so are you. I want you to have it." They hugged one another and went to bed, though neither was sure she could sleep after the night they'd had.

Within a few days, the crops began to thrive, and the villagers were able to feed themselves and their families once again. The long, agonizing drought had finally come to an end. No more would the people starve or suffer through sickness that could be cured with the right herbs.

Phoenix had never been so proud or felt so useful as she did the day of the harvest. The townspeople gathered together, rejoicing in the good news. She looked over the crowd, sighing happily. *I don't see how anyone could turn their backs on the craft,* she thought. *This is wondrous.*

****

As she sat beneath the tree, thinking back on that day, she smiled. A warm feeling flowed through her, and her cheeks were flushed. Nothing else ever came close to bringing her such joy as the feeling of helping others and making a difference in the world.

"Beautiful," said a voice from beside her. Rodrick Finnegan… he had a smile that could make any girl's heart race, and his eyes sparkled like the sea.

Well, almost nothing. She reached her hand up so that her suitor could help her to her feet. He had been courting her for a few months, and she had begun to envision their lives together. It just felt right. They were so close and so comfortable around each other.

They could truly be themselves when together, which was not always easy for Phoenix. She often had to force herself into social situations. She enjoyed having friends and feeling connected to others, but there were many times that she would much prefer to stay home, snuggled beneath the hearth with a good book.

She wrapped her arms around Rodrick's and walked with him through the field. "Sorcha, come!" she called out to her little sister, the brunette with the pigtails and dimples.

"Aww, do we have to?" Sorcha shouted, her arms dropping to her side in exasperation. "We were having so much fun, and the sun's not even setting yet?"

Phoenix smiled and held out her hand for her sister to join her. "I know, dear sister, but tonight is the Town Hall meeting, so dinner will be early. You know how mother gets when we are late."

Sorcha relented, knowing that her sister was right. That was one of her worst qualities, as far as Sorcha was concerned. *Just once, I would like to win an argument with her.* She joined Phoenix and Rodrick, holding her sister's hand as they made their way home.

The two lovebirds exchanged looks, and Sorcha rolled her eyes. At that point, she wasn't sure she could stomach dinner. She was barely able to keep her lunch down as it was. *Ugh, romance,* she thought to herself, kicking a rock as they walked.

****

They were not always so close. In fact, Phoenix had been wary of him at first. She'd had many a suitor offer their hand, but none of them had the best of intentions. Some only courted her because their parents were friends and it was expected. Others wanted to be the one to get the "shy girl" to come out of her shell, yet they could never understand her or her interests.

They would always ask her why she couldn't be more "normal." She never wanted to be normal, though. If normal meant hurting those who were different from you and getting caught up in superficial nonsense, then that wasn't something that would ever interest her.

Because of her experiences with these suitors, she was less than accepting when Rodrick showed interest. The only reason she even considered getting to know him was that her best friend, Constance, had suggested it. "You need to get out more. You can't always have your nose buried in a book."

However, Phoenix still was unsure. She gave in, but she kept her guard up, just in case. She figured there must be something he was getting out of it, and it certainly wasn't her company. Oh, how wrong she was.

It was a slow start, but he gradually earned her trust. She never cared about gifts or fancy dates, and he knew that. He took her on picnics beneath her favorite tree and horseback rides through the meadow. He focused on spending time with her and getting to know her, rather than trying to impress her and making it all about him like the others did.

He would surprise her with beautiful rocks he found throughout each day. "They sparkle like your eyes," he would tell her. "So, I thought that you should have them." He would bring her books from her favorite authors and her favorite flowers.

She looked at him with such love in her eyes. It was the little things like that – things that showed he listened to her – that let her know how much he truly cared.

When they started dating more and more, he noticed that Constance had begun to get jealous. So, he invited her along during some of their picnics and even set up fun activities for the girls to do alone... Phoenix, Constance, and Sorcha.

"Are you sure?" she asked. "I thought you wanted us to spend time together tonight."

"I never want you to feel like you have to choose between me and your friends and family," he said, running his hand through her crimson hair. "You are free to spend your time with whomever you'd like."

"Of course, I want to spend time with you."

"And I, you. I am honored to be part of your life, and I cherish our time together, but I know that nothing can compare to the connection between sisters or even best friends. You should be with them as well. We have plenty of time to spend together. We can do something tomorrow night. Now, go. Have fun."

She kissed him on his cheek, then left with Constance and Sorcha. They had a wonderful time together, just as they always had. Though Rodrick was not there, her heart began to race as she felt herself growing more and more in love with him.

There was a strong connection between them, and they seemed to share many of the same interests. More than that, they took a real, genuine interest in one another... as people, as friends, as potential lovers. They cared very deeply about one another's well-being... both physical and emotional. It was unlike anything she had ever experienced.

****

They continued walking through the field and onward toward the Doyle Estate... the sisters' family farm. Phoenix looked down at her little sister, swinging their arms back and forth and twirling Sorcha as she danced about. The two of them often fought, as siblings do, but they truly were the best of friends. When push came to shove, they were always there for one another, and they enjoyed the time they spent together.

Forever Changed

They had almost made it home when Phoenix stopped short and turned her gaze toward her house. Feeling a knot in her stomach, she began to panic. Her breathing became sporadic. Something was wrong.

"What is the matter?" asked Rodrick, concerned. "Are you all right?"

She couldn't speak – the fear building up within her was holding her captive. All she could bring herself to do was shake her head. She let go of their hands and ran the rest of the way up the hill to her house, bursting through the door. Her parents were curled up together on the couch, her father's arms wrapped lovingly around her mother's shoulders. They looked up at her with sadness in their eyes.

"What's wrong?" she asked, not sure that she wanted the answer.

By then, Rodrick and Sorcha had joined her, and they looked around the room, wondering what had happened.

The girls' mother opened her mouth to respond, then stopped. "I can't," she said. "I can't do it." She burst into tears and stood, walking over to the side so as to not let anyone see the pain she was fighting so hard to hold in. It was not the time to lose herself. She had to be strong for her girls. She covered her hand with her mouth and closed her eyes, trying to compose herself.

Phoenix began to hyperventilate. *This is bad, really bad.* She wouldn't admit to herself what she already knew. She turned to face her father, desperation in her eyes. She hoped beyond hope that it was something – anything – other than what she felt in her heart to be true.

He struggled for a moment before finally speaking. "It's your grandmother."

"NO!" Phoenix shouted, her hands covering her mouth. "It can't... she can't!" She ran to her grandmother's room, where the doctor was preparing to move her body. She stood in the doorway, her mouth agape as she struggled to breathe. Tears flowed down her pale face as she felt the world slipping away.

She could not imagine life without her beloved grandmother, the woman she admired more than anyone in the world. She had influenced her life so greatly. How could she possibly go on without her?

She watched as her grandmother's body was placed on a stretcher and carried out by the doctor and his nurse. As they carried her grandmother out of her room for the last time, Phoenix reached over and ran her hand through her hair and across her face.

Feeling the coldness of her grandmother's skin on her hand, she fell against the door and sat on the floor, sobbing hysterically. Rodrick rushed over and held his beloved, consoling her as best he could. Sorcha held onto her mother, crying and not wanting to look as her grandmother was carried out the front door.

Their father walked over and embraced Sorcha and her mother, doing his best to comfort them. Constance had been walking by when she saw what happened. "Oh, no" she whispered, then ran into the house. "Phoenix?" she called out, and Mr. Doyle pointed down the hallway toward his daughter. Constance ran over and kneeled down next to her, wrapping her arms around her friend as she sobbed into her shoulder.

Their family was forever changed. Grandmother Lorna had been a constant in their lives, always there for them. She had taught Phoenix so much, but she still had so much left to teach her.

How could she be gone already? She wasn't even all that old. She was still bristling with life and energy when Phoenix and Sorcha had left for the field. How could she have passed so suddenly? It didn't make sense to her. She was sure that it must be a dream. *Please, let it be a dream.*

Saying Goodbye

The family arrived at the cemetery and huddled together near the coffin. Phoenix couldn't bear the thought of her grandmother being trapped in that pine wood box, but she wasn't. It was only her body. Her soul was free. She had moved on. Phoenix was sure of it. There had to be more than the life they lived on this earth. It was one of the few things she truly believed from the stories she read in the Bible. She just was not so sure their definitions of the afterlife were the same.

Rodrick wrapped his arms around her in an attempt to comfort her. She knew he meant well, and she did appreciate his warmth and kindness, but all she really wanted was her grandmother back. She felt a gnawing pain deep within her stomach. It had been there since the day of her grandmother's passing. She couldn't imagine that it would ever cease. It was as if a piece of her very soul had died along with Grandmother Lorna.

She looked at her mother and sister; both were crying just as much as she, though she doubted either of them shared the same connection with her. There was no doubt they loved her and were hurting, and she felt guilty for the thought that her pain was different than theirs.

However, she knew that what they shared as witches was stronger than anything else she had experienced; it was a connection that transcended all others. It was completely indescribable. They had done something together that no one knew was even possible. They had healed the lands together and saved people from sickness and death.

Now, Grandmother was gone, and she did not know how she could bear to continue her lessons without the only person from whom she wanted to learn... the only person who *could* teach her. All that she had left of her was the book she'd given her. It was only fitting that Grandmother Lorna should have something that connected them as well.

She rubbed the carnation her grandmother had given her, then removed it. As the coffin was lowered into the ground, Phoenix tossed the flower on top. "Goodbye, Grandmother. I love you."

The other mourners followed suit, tossing flowers onto the coffin before parting ways. The bells chimed as they exited the cemetery. With each chime of the bell, Phoenix felt another crack in her fragile heart.

The rest of the mourners somberly returned to their homes. Then, once they arrived, they hung up their coats and went about their days as usual. That was the farthest thing from Phoenix's mind. *How can they all act like today is just any other day? It isn't. Nothing's the same. Nothing will ever be the same again.*

The Birthday

A month had passed since Grandmother's passing, and the family was preparing to celebrate Sorcha's eleventh birthday. They would have a picnic in the field and invite all her friends to attend. Their mother was baking a cake, and family members were all pitching in, each of them bringing a special dish.

Everything seemed to be going well until Sorcha burst through the door, slamming it behind her. "Cancel the picnic. I don't want to celebrate my birthday anymore!"

"Sorcha? What's wrong? Are you okay?"

"No, I'm not okay! Isla is my best friend, and now she's not coming! She never comes around anymore, but I thought she would at least come today." She burst into tears, her little shoulders shaking as she sobbed.

Phoenix kneeled down in front of her sister and put her arms on her shoulders, but Sorcha pulled away and glared at her. "Honey, what happened? Why is your friend not coming?"

"Because of you! That's why! She won't come because of you. Why couldn't you just be normal?" With that, Sorcha ran to her room and threw herself onto her bed, sobbing into her pillow.

Phoenix stood there, dumbfounded. How could this be her fault? She hadn't done anything to the girl. Could this really be because she was so different from everyone else? Why should that matter? Besides, she had always been different. She would have thought Isla and her family would be used to it by now. She didn't know what she did to offend them, but she would find out. She would make things right.

As her mother attempted to console Sorcha, Phoenix left the house in search of Isla. They did not live far, so she was sure she would have the situation resolved and bring the girl back with her before the cake was finished.

She arrived at the Sullivan estate a short time later and knocked on the door. A moment passed before it opened, revealing Isla's mother. Before Phoenix could utter a word, the woman scowled at her and chastised her harshly, saying, "Your kind is not wanted here."

"Who is it, dear?"

Isla's father came to the door, and his wife gestured toward Phoenix angrily. He nodded, and she went back inside to her family. "What do you want?"

"I am sorry to bother you, but I was hoping that your daughter could join us in the field near our estate for my sister's birthday."

"Absolutely not!"

"I am sorry if I offended you in some way. If there is any way to reconcile that, I would be happy to, but they really are the best of friends. Surely, you cannot object to Isla coming for just a little while."

"I most certainly can object, and I do. I admit, I am fond of little Sorcha, and she is welcome here anytime. However, I will not have my daughter associating with the likes of you… witch!"

Phoenix felt as if she had been punched in the gut. She stood there, motionless, as Mr. Sullivan closed the door. She turned slowly and looked out at the onlookers who had overheard the conversation. They stared at her as they whispered amongst themselves.

Her head began to spin, and she sensed danger looming ahead. She ran home as quickly as her legs could carry her. She apologized to Sorcha and told the family to go on and celebrate without her. Her mother objected, but Phoenix insisted.

"Listen, it is really important to me that Sorcha has her best friend with her, and if I am the reason that she cannot come, then I should not be there. I know that I would be devastated if I could not spend my birthday with Rodrick or Constance. I will celebrate with her later, but for now… let her have her time with friends."

Her mother nodded slightly, then hugged her. They finished the preparations and sent Sorcha to collect her friend. Then they went to the field, leaving Phoenix behind.

She lay on her bed, looking up at the ceiling. *How could everything go so wrong? How did they find out? I don't understand. What's so wrong with witches anyway?* She turned over and pulled her pillow toward her, hugging it. *I wish you were here, Grandmother. You would know what to do.*

After the party, the family returned home. Phoenix, having fallen asleep, awoke to the sound of her bedroom door closing. Her mother stood there with her hands behind her back. "We need to talk," she said.

"What is the matter?"

"Are…" She paused for a moment, collecting her thoughts and trying to refrain from yelling. "Did your grandmother give you this?" She revealed what was hiding behind her back… the book of magick.

"Where did you get that? It was…"

"In your nightstand, I know. I found it in there just before you awoke."

"Why were you looking?"

"I didn't want to believe it. I really didn't. When they told me that you were a witch and accused me of being one... I nearly collapsed then and there. How could you keep this from me?"

"Grandmother said that you wanted no part of magick."

"So, she went behind my back and taught it to you? To my own daughter?"

"No, it wasn't like that. I found the book on my own. It was tucked away in the attic... the attic that you sent me to clean."

"Do not put this on me. It never should have been there in the first place. She should have gotten rid of it long ago."

"Why would she do that? It was such a huge part of her. Magick was a part of her, and she was a great person. How could you be so ashamed of that?"

"I know that she was an incredible woman, and I loved her so much, but this... this is unholy." She turned and walked toward the living room.

"Mother? What... what are you doing? Mother, no!" She followed her, fear taking over. "What are you going to do?" She watched helplessly as her mother threw the book into the fireplace. "NO! Mother, no! Why would you do that? That was all that I had left of Grandmother!"

"And now there is nothing. Nothing of my mother's shall remain in this house. She brought damnation upon us, and we will not honor that, no matter how much we may love her."

"No, this isn't love. Love doesn't turn its back on the people who matter most and who care for us. Love doesn't hurt others or hate them for who they truly are. You may hate witchcraft, but that doesn't mean that it doesn't exist or even that it shouldn't. I will never be ashamed of Grandmother. I would be proud to be half the woman she was. Shame on you for thinking otherwise!"

Her mother raised her hand, slapping her across the face. "Do not speak to me in that manner, child. You are my daughter, and you will show me respect."

Anger boiling inside of her, Phoenix thought it best to leave before she did something she might regret. So, she grabbed her shawl and walked out the door. She wasn't sure where she was going, but she knew she couldn't stay there.

The Accused

As Phoenix walked through the streets, she was caught off-guard by a man shouting at her. "There she is... the witch!"

A woman nearby cried out, "It's her! Protect the children!"

More cries emanated from the villagers as they left the comfort of their own homes to see what the commotion was all about. Phoenix turned every which way, seeing villagers gather all around her, pointing their fingers as they made their accusations.

A tingling sensation crept down her spine, and her heart began to flutter. Her cheeks were flushed, and her breathing intensified. Tears rolled down her cheeks as she realized that the entire village – her home, her friends, her family – had turned against her. She was all alone in the world. Having lost everyone and everything that mattered to her, she collapsed in the street.

Rodrick walked up around that time and saw her lying in the street while everyone hurled insults at her. He pushed past them and lifted her up, taking her into his home. He lay her on the sofa and tried to wake her. When she did not awaken, he placed a mirror by her nose to make sure that she was breathing.

Relieved, he hugged her tightly, then grabbed her some blankets. He hoped that she was okay. He knew not what was happening, but he would not ask the others. He did not like the way they were treating his beloved, and he did not want to risk unleashing his anger on them if they insulted her to his face.

He spent the night looking after her, just to be sure. He pulled his chair closer and ran his fingers through her hair, looking at her with such love. He thought her to be so beautiful and kind and loving. He couldn't imagine anyone wishing her harm.

The next morning, Phoenix woke with a start. She looked around, trying to make sense of things. It took her a moment to realize where she was. She turned and saw Rodrick in his chair, where he had finally fallen asleep sometime during the night.

"Rodrick?" she called to him. When he didn't respond, she lightly shook his leg. "Rodrick, wake up."

He stirred for a moment before waking. "Phoenix, are you all right?"

She nodded slightly. "What happened?"

"I don't know. I found you in the street, unconscious. I brought you in here to make sure you were safe. It took a while for everyone to go back home. When they did, I went to your house to get your parents, but they turned me away. What happened? Why is everyone so angry with you?"

"Oh, Rodrick. It's simply awful..." Before she could continue, there was a knock at the door. She looked toward it, her eyes widening as she braced herself for the worst.

Rodrick saw the worry in her eyes and looked back and forth between her and the door before finally standing and answering it. "Can I help you?" he asked as he stood in the doorway, facing the local minister.

"I understand that you have Miss Doyle here with you."

"Oh, yes, but it is not like that. You see..."

The minister cut him off with a wave of his hand. "I do not know how to tell you this, but your companion has been accused of witchcraft." Rodrick turned toward Phoenix with a puzzled look on his face.

"Rodrick, please…"

"Listen, there must be some mistake," he said, not wanting to believe the accusations.

"I wish that it were," said the minister. "Unfortunately, we have evidence that supports the accusations, and Miss Doyle will stand trial. She must be brought in at once."

Rodrick looked at Phoenix with concern. He wanted to yell at the minister and slam the door in his face, but he could not. He hoped that his cooperation would grant him the time he needed to find out the truth and help his beloved Phoenix. At the very least, it would allow him the chance to attend the trial and perhaps testify on her behalf. If he were to make a scene, he would not be afforded such an opportunity.

Reluctantly, he stepped back while the minister signaled for the others to join him. As the magistrates entered the house, Phoenix tried to move out of their reach. Unfortunately, she was not able to move quickly enough, and they grabbed her.

"Rodrick, please help me."

"I'm sorry. I will do what I can. We will figure this out. Just be good and cooperate. Everything will be okay, I promise."

The Betrayal

The trial was rushed, as charges of witchcraft were taken quite seriously following the executions in Europe. Tales of possessions, specters, and fits were spread throughout the village by recent newcomers. The trial was presided over by the local magistrate, Declan McCarthy, as well as Archibald Wallace and Artúr Finnegan, Rodrick's father.

"The witches are wreaking havoc across the country," testified a Frenchman, Guillaume de Lorraine, who had arrived in America a year earlier. "Their works have become so sinister that cases of lycanthropy have emerged. We cannot allow them to cross into our territory and inflict the same damage. We must heed the Bible's warning. As the scripture says, 'Thou shalt not suffer a witch to live!'"

Cheers erupted from the crowd, followed by jeers directed at Phoenix. McCarthy called for order and thanked the Frenchman. "You are dismissed."

When asked for further witnesses, the court called upon Isla. She stood and looked around the room, pushing back her hair and straightening her dress. As she walked past Phoenix, she grew nervous and did her best to keep her distance. She took her seat as directed, placing her hand upon the Bible and swearing to tell the truth, the whole truth, and nothing but the truth... so help her God.

Phoenix rolled her eyes, trying to refrain from laughing at that line. *Some God,* she thought. *What kind of God orders his children to kill each other, just for existing? What kind of God sees somebody with great power – somebody who uses that power to help others and heal the earth – and decides that they are not worthy? That they do not deserve the same love and respect as everyone else? That they deserve to die?*

Wallace looked at Isla, calming his voice and leaning in to speak to her. "Would you tell the court what you told your parents?"

Isla glanced over at Phoenix and took a deep breath. She closed her eyes for a moment, reminding herself of all the lessons she had learned in Sunday school and of all the stories that everyone had told her. She thought of the good work her parents told her she was doing and how she would be making God happy. That was what they told her, so it had to be true.

Finally, ready to face the court, she opened her eyes. "Phoenix is a witch."

She lowered her head, not wanting the court to see her cry. She could not show weakness – not now, not when her life was on the line. She had to be strong and stay alert, just in case. She just hoped at least some of the townspeople knew her well enough to take her side. She may be a witch, but she had never done anything to harm anyone. Surely, they couldn't think that she was a threat.

"How do you know that she is a witch? Did someone tell you that?"

"No. I saw it myself."

Gasps of horror and frenzied chatter flooded the courtroom. The jury huddled together, whispering as they stared at Phoenix. She could not believe what she was hearing. Isla was lying. She had to be. There was no way she had ever seen her use witchcraft. Her parents must have put her up to this, but how could they have known? None of it made any sense to her.

She looked desperately at her parents, silently begging them to help her. Her father pulled her mother closer, and their heads touched as they averted their eyes. The whispers died out as McCarthy waved his hand.

"You saw it?"

"Yes, your honor."

"When did you see it?"

"Before the miracle happened – when God sent his angels to save us. When the fields were bare and the crops were dead, I saw her… and her grandmother."

"And what did you see them doing?"

"It was late at night. I was spending the night with Sorcha. We were having a sleepover…"

"Isla, how could you?!" shouted Sorcha, now standing in the aisle. "You swore you wouldn't say anything!"

"I'm sorry, Sorcha. I had no choice. I was scared."

"Order! Order! Lassie, do you know something about this? I will remind you that you are in a courtroom, standing before God. What say ye?"

Sorcha began to panic, looking out at the townspeople. She knew not what to do. She could not bear the thought of turning her sister in, but she also couldn't lie. She looked at her sister with eyes full of guilt and sorrow.

Phoenix stood and walked over to Sorcha and kneeled down before her. Her mother tried to grab her, but she pulled away. She turned back to face her sister, tucking loose strands of hair behind her ear.

"There are those beautiful eyes," she said, wiping away a tear from her own face. "Listen, everything will be okay.

Whatever you have to say, say it. I do not blame you for what is happening, and I never want you to think that this is your fault. Never be afraid to speak your truth, no matter what anyone tells you or how anyone feels about what you have to say. Be true to yourself."

Sorcha nodded, and they embraced one another. Their parents rose to their feet and pulled Sorcha away. "That's enough. Your honor, might we have a moment so that Sorcha can collect her thoughts?"

"There had better not be any foul play. I expect complete cooperation."

"Of course, your honor."

"Very well, then."

Phoenix stood, and McCarthy ordered her to take a seat. "You will have your turn." Everyone shifted their focus back to Isla. "Now, what were you saying?"

She exchanged worried looks with her friend, then looked at Phoenix, who simply nodded. She took another deep breath, then continued. "We didn't know what they were doing at first. We weren't trying to cause any trouble, I promise. We just... we heard them rummaging around in the attic and then sneaking out to the barn. So, we followed them."

"And what did you see when you followed them out there?"

"They were huddled over a big pot."

"A big pot? Do you mean a cauldron?" asked Finnegan.

"Yes, I suppose."

"Continue."

As Phoenix listened to Isla's testimony, she realized that the girls had been out there the night they healed the lands and ended the drought. *They made the noise. I knew someone was there. We only thought it was the cat.*

"Well, they were putting herbs and other ingredients in the pot and whispering chants."

"What sort of chants, lass?"

"I don't know. They weren't in any language that I ever knew."

"I see, and are the rest of the Doyle family witches as well?"

"No, your honor. I asked Sorcha that, but she denied it."

"Are you certain that she was not lying?"

"Oh, yes, absolutely certain. She would never lie to me. We're best friends." She hung her head low, feeling ashamed for having betrayed that friendship. "She was as confused by all of this as I was."

"Then why did she ask you to hide this secret from the rest of us?"

"Because she loved her sister… and her grandmother. And they would never hurt anyone. I don't know why I was so afraid. You just hear so many stories, and you aren't sure what to believe. I'm sorry, Sorcha… and Phoenix. I'm so sorry."

More hushed chatter spread across the room, and Wallace addressed Isla once more. "Lass, it is quite all right. You did nothing wrong. Miss Doyle and her grandmother did. As you well know, witchcraft is forbidden in the eyes of the Lord. Do you understand this?"

"Yes, sir."

"We must keep our distance from such things. You may feel conflicted right now, but in time you will understand. For your safety and your family's, you must be wary."

Isla nodded.

"Now, before I dismiss you, is there anything else you can tell us that will help?"

"Not really… oh, they did put the potion into bottles."

"I see, and what did they do with these bottles?"

"They left. I wanted to follow, but Sorcha was afraid we would get caught."

"So, even your young friend was afraid of her own family?"

"No, it wasn't like that. She was afraid that we would get caught out of bed. As I said, it was late at night, and we were meant to be sleeping."

"Ah, continue."

"The last I saw of them that night, they were heading out toward the farmlands. We ran back inside and went to bed, neither of us wanting to speak of what we had witnessed."

"Aye. Well, thank you again, lass. You may be seated," he said, gesturing. She rose to her feet and once again joined her family.

A Family Divided

Next, they called upon Phoenix's mother. "Mrs. Doyle, I apologize for the pain and suffering your family is enduring, but I must ask for your testimony as well... as difficult as it may be."

She nodded slowly while dabbing away at her tears with a kerchief. "Aye." She sniffled, then continued, "I understand, though I don't know what help I can be, your honor. I knew not of my daughter's involvement with witchcraft before the accusations began. That is not something I ever would have condoned."

Phoenix felt her face flush. She felt so alone in the world... and so guilty. She hated disappointing her parents. She never meant to cause them pain. She never meant for any of this to happen, but how could she deny a part of herself – especially such a large part of herself and her family's history? How could she turn a blind eye, knowing that her power could be used to end everyone's suffering?

"And what of your mother?" asked Finnegan.

"Well, she was a stubborn old woman, very set in her ways. She was taught that witchcraft would set her free, that it could be used for good."

"It can, mother!" shouted Phoenix. Whispers once again erupted from the townspeople, and McCarthy ordered silence. "Miss Doyle, you shall sit down at once. You will have your chance soon enough. For now, it is your mother's time to speak." He gave Phoenix one more scowl before turning back to Fiona. "Now, as you were saying..."

"Well, my mother practiced witchcraft most of her life, and she always hoped that I would join her, but I refused."

"I see, and why did you never speak of this before?"

"Well, she was my mother. I was torn between my duty as a child of God and my obligation to honor my mother and father. Plus, I had hoped that she would see the error in her ways. When she grew older and my father passed on, we invited her to live with us, but I told her that if she were to join our family, witchcraft had to be a thing of the past. She could not bring those unholy works into my home. She agreed, and I had no idea that rather than throw it out as I demanded, she had simply hidden it away in our attic, where my daughter eventually found it."

As the day went on, more and more townspeople testified against her, some proclaiming outright lies. Collette O'Reilly and her friends made up stories of persecution, pretending to be victims of Phoenix's craft. They claimed to be suffering from a multitude of ailments and hallucinations, all at the hands of Phoenix. Each story was more ridiculous than the last, and yet the townspeople believed it all.

Phoenix grew tense with worry. She had never before been so uncertain of the future. She wished that Rodrick were there, holding her hand and telling her that everything would be all right. She kept glancing at the door, hoping that he would eventually show. When he didn't, she felt the very last ounce of courage resolve. She truly was alone in the world, and now she would die that way.

Finally, it was her turn to speak. She was led to the witness stand. She braced herself for the questions she knew were coming.

"Miss Doyle, what say you?"

"What do you want me to say?"

"Are you a witch, Miss Doyle?"

She thought for a moment. As she looked out over the crowd, she realized that she had a choice. She could admit the truth and face certain death, or she could lie and possibly avoid conviction. However, she knew that would only provide false hope, and she knew that she could not deny her true self or turn her back on her grandmother. Dead or alive, she would not betray her.

"Yes. I am a witch."

The Verdict

Before sentencing, they allowed her to continue her testimony. "Though we have all the evidence we need and a confession, I would like to hear what she has to say," said McCarthy as the crowd grew restless. "Continue, Miss Doyle."

"As I said, I am a witch, but that does not mean that I am evil."

"Actually, that is precisely what it means!" shouted Finnegan. "Witchcraft is evil, and so is anyone who practices it. You bring it into our village and our lives. You go to school with our children. You seduce our sons and influence our daughters. You used your magic on my son, didn't you? You cast some spell to make him fall for you!"

"That is not true! Don't you realize what we were doing that night in the barn? We were saving all of you! You would be dead if not for us and our craft."

"That is a lie!" shouted a woman in the back of the room.

"Quiet down. What do you mean by this, Miss Doyle?"

"The drought…"

"The drought you and your coven of witches no doubt inflicted upon us all."

"No, it isn't like that. I wasn't even alive when it started."

"But your grandmother was."

"Yes, and if she'd had any idea how to end it, she would have. I was the one who figured it out. It was my idea to go out there that night. We both wanted so desperately to help everyone. We couldn't bear the sight of people dying of starvation and pestilence... especially knowing that we had this power and that there must be some way to help.

So, I found a way. I studied and studied, learning about herbs and their magickal properties. I studied the soil and read as much as I could until I was certain I had found the way. Grandmother was only too happy to lend a helping hand. So, we went out to the barn with our ingredients and our cauldron, and we brewed a potion. We recited our incantations, as Isla said. That is true.

But then we went out to the farmlands and the fields, and we used that potion to restore life to the earth and to help the crops thrive so that we all might live... so that *you* all might live. We did not curse you. We saved you!"

"Witch!" shouted Mrs. O'Connor, a neighbor woman from down the street.

"Yes, I believe that we have already established that much," said Wallace.

"No!" shouted the woman again. "You do not understand. She may have tried to save us, but in doing so, she did curse us. She has damned us all to hell!"

The townspeople gasped in horror, looking about the room in terror. "What do you mean by this?" asked Finnegan.

"She used that vile potion on our crops... our food, that we might partake of it. Don't you see? She has forced us to consume the product of her witchcraft. She has poisoned us all, and now we have feasted upon the devil's brew. We are all doomed to hell for eternity. We shall never see the gates of Heaven now that she has inflicted us all with her witchcraft."

Panic ensued as the townspeople realized that she was right… they had all unknowingly consumed the potion through their food. Their lives may have been saved, but their souls would surely perish.

"You have sacrificed us all. Have you no shame?"

"This is ridiculous! Magick isn't evil. It can be used for good! That is all that I was trying to do!"

"Do you know what witchcraft is?" asked McCarthy with a grave expression on his face. "It is the work of the devil himself. He feeds off the good intentions of young souls such as yourself. He corrupts them, and he has corrupted you. You may have intended to help us all, but you have caused far more harm than any drought or disease ever could. You have effectively damned all our souls to spend eternity in hell, just as you shall. It is by order of the court that Miss Doyle shall be burned at the stake… tomorrow!"

Hope Shattered

Phoenix was taken from the courtroom and out to the center of town so that everyone could witness her being put in the stocks. The crowd jeered and pelted her with random objects. They shouted obscenities at her. Though most of them had been quite reserved in the past, they now felt as though they no longer had anything to lose.

WITCH! WITCH! WITCH! WITCH! WITCH!

The shouting and abuse continued throughout the day, until the late hours of the night when the crowd finally died out, leaving her all alone with her thoughts. Until then, she had held onto hope that all would be well… the townspeople would see her for who she truly was and realize that witchcraft was not the great evil they thought it was. How foolish she had been. At that moment, she knew. They would never understand.

With silence all around and nothing but a few nocturnal animals to keep her company, she allowed herself to feel every ounce of pain and fear that she had been trying so hard to keep buried deep inside. She choked out the initial sobs and screamed, her entire body shaking as she wailed.

Why is this happening to me? What did I ever do to deserve this? Oh, Grandmother. I wish that you were here to guide me.

"Phoenix?" a voice called out.

"Grandmother?"

"No, silly. It's me."

"Constance! And Rodrick? What are you two doing here?"

"We've come to save you," said Rodrick. "What else?"

"I thought you had abandoned me."

"Why would I do that?"

"Because… they say that I am evil and that my very existence curses them."

"They are wrong. I am so sorry I was not there with you. I couldn't risk it. You know how my father is. Besides, if I stood in their way or testified on your behalf, I would be right here alongside you, and I knew that would do you no good. I had to find Constance and come up with a plan. They may think you are some witch, but we know the truth."

"But you don't understand. They're not wrong. I am a witch."

Constance and Rodrick stopped what they were doing and looked at each other, then at her. "What?" they asked in unison.

"No, that can't be," said Rodrick.

"I'm sorry. I should have told you the truth. I never should have let you fall in love with me."

"Wait, are you saying – did you use your power to force me to love you?"

"NO! I would never do that! The only magick that I use is light magick. I tried to help. I… I healed the land and revived the crops so that no others would perish, but I fear that has only made them hate me more."

"I don't understand," said Constance. "If you saved them – saved us – then why would they hate you for that?"

"They say that I have doomed you all by allowing you to eat food tainted with my magick and that you all will be damned to hell. I am so sorry."

Constance thought for a moment before replying, "Don't be. They are wrong. God would not punish someone for something they had no control over; neither would he damn a soul who was only trying to save the lives of her people.

"What you did was incredible! I have never known there to be anyone with the ability to wield such power and yet use it for good... to heal rather than hurt. That... is not evil. There is goodness inside of you, and if I can see that, so can God. I have to believe that. Otherwise, what is point in believing in the first place?"

"I love you, Connie."

"I love you too, Phoenix. You are like the sister I always wanted, and I will not let you die!" She grabbed a rock and began to smash the locks... two, three, and four times... until finally it smashed open and dropped to the ground.

Phoenix gasped. She never expected that to work. She looked up at Rodrick's equally-stunned face. "Run!" he shouted. And they did.

They ran and ran, as fast as their legs could carry them. They knew not where they were headed... only that they could not stay in their village. "The mountains," whispered Constance. "We can hide in the mountains." The others nodded and followed her.

Unfortunately, they never made it. Guards were patrolling the village to ensure the witch did not escape or harm any of the townspeople. They heard the three approach and grabbed them. "No! Let us go!" shouted Phoenix. "Please! We won't hurt anyone. I just want my freedom!"

"And now you are all in trouble. Come, McCarthy and the others should be made aware of this."

Phoenix, Rodrick, and Constance were taken before the council for questioning. "What were you doing with my son, you witch?!" shouted Finnegan, standing mere inches away from her face, his own turning red with anger.

"Father, stop!" yelled Rodrick, pulling at his arm. "We helped her escape. It was our plan, not hers."

"Why would you do such a thing? She's a witch!"

"I know, father."

"You – you do? How could you keep that from me? Are you in league with her – with the devil?"

"Would you listen to yourself? I didn't know she was a witch until tonight. She confessed, but I saved her anyway because I know who she truly is. She just wants her freedom. She deserves it. She didn't harm anyone. She saved us. Please, let her go."

His father turned around and covered his mouth with his hand, deep in thought; he took a few steps a shook his head before turning back. "No, I cannot allow this. It's witchcraft, son! She is a witch, and no good can come of that. Don't you understand? She has damned us all to hell by forcing us to partake in that devil's brew she concocted. Now, our only hope at grace is to follow God's orders and make her pay for her crimes. Get her out of here! And you, son, should go home. This no longer concerns you."

"Father, no! Wait, please!" Rodrick cried out as the guards grabbed Phoenix and took her away.

"Go home at once! I will not repeat myself a third time. If you disobey me again, I will be forced to try you for treason."

Rodrick stood there, stunned. He could not believe his father could be cold and heartless. Anger building up inside of him, he stormed out.

Finnegan turned back toward the others, and McCarthy cleared his throat as he made preparations. "Wallace, take Miss Doyle's young friend here home. Her parents will be worried."

"No, you can't do this! She's my best friend. Please don't hurt her."

"She is nobody's friend. Goodnight, Miss Reid." Screams echoed through the town as the trio were torn apart, each taken their separate ways as the town made their preparations.

Judgement Day

Phoenix walked through the town with shackles binding her hands together. She tried desperately to keep her balance as the guards dragged her along, eager to be rid of the witch. She ambled quietly along, no longer able to cry or scream or beg. Every ounce of hope that had remained throughout the whole ordeal was now gone.

She looked out into the crowd and saw Rodrick and Constance, their faces wrinkled with worry. She turned and saw her sister, Sorcha, whose eyes were filled with tears. Behind her stood their parents, who looked at her as though she were a stranger.

"Mother, father!" she cried out. "Please... help me!"

Her father averted his gaze and rubbed his wife's shoulder before parting. "I'm sorry. I can't be here for this." Her mother looked her in the eye and said, "I never wanted this. I never wanted any of this for you... but you made your choice."

"No. No, mother please!" Her heart shattered. As angry as her mother was, she never imagined that she could stand there and watch as her own daughter was tormented. Had she ever loved her?

The guards continued dragging her along until they finally reached the stake. The shackles were removed, and Phoenix was pushed against the large, wooden beam as Wallace and Finnegan tied her arms and legs to it. Once finished, Wallace took his place alongside the others. Finnegan pulled on the ropes to make sure they were tight enough. "We wouldn't want you escaping again."

"Please don't do this. I never meant any of you harm. I was trying to help… to end your suffering. Why does that deserve punishment?"

"Because you are a witch, and you used your dark magick on us."

"I used my power for good. That is all."

"And what about the girls you tormented?"

"They're lying! I never harmed them."

"I very much doubt they're the ones lying."

"They are."

"Even so… you have brought this upon yourself with your heresy."

"I helped you, and now you all have forsaken me. You can't do this to me! I won't allow it! Let me go!" She tried her best to break free of the ropes that bound her but to no avail. She twisted and turned every which way and even tried to hit Finnegan with her head, but he stepped back.

"Ooh, you have a bit of fire in you, don't you lass? You sure do put up a fight when you have to." He leaned closer and whispered into her ear. "Too bad your grandmother didn't."

"No. You. YOU!" she shouted, rage boiling up inside of her. "You killed her! How could you?!"

"Goodbye, Miss Doyle."

"Oh, you call me evil. You are the one who is evil, and you have not yet seen dark magick and what it can do! You will suffer for what you have done; you can be certain of that."

"Is that so? Well, we'll see." With that, he nodded to the executioners. Phoenix screamed and struggled to break free, but it was of no use. The executioners each grabbed their torches and set fire to the stake. Phoenix looked out at the crowd and saw Sorcha clinging to her mother, unable to bear the sight of her sister in pain.

Guards held back Rodrick and Constance, who were trying desperately to break free. "Please!" shouted Constance. "We have to help her! Don't do this!"

Phoenix looked up at the sky and closed her eyes, finally accepting her fate. She began chanting:

Relinquo hoc mundo
Sed revertar
Inimici mei erit pati
Idem tormentum et nocentibus
Ego resurget semel
Ut mei nominis habet

A single tear rolled down her cheek, and she let out a loud, agonizing scream as the flames engulfed her.

The Reckoning

The flames faded away, and all that remained were her ashes. Once they were certain that she was dead, they let go of Rodrick and Constance, then dismissed the crowd. Everyone went back to their homes and their businesses.

Rodrick hugged Constance as she wept. "How can they pretend that nothing happened?" she asked. "How can they just kill someone and not even care?"

"I don't know, but they will pay for what they've done. God will see to that. She didn't deserve to die. I don't care what the Bible says. The God I believe in would never wish this horror on someone so… perfect. She never hurt anyone. She helped us, and this is how they show their gratitude? I won't stand for this."

"What are you going to do?"

"I don't know, but there has to be something we can do. People like that should not be in power. Killing the innocent… that is not justice."

They looked back once more at the stake, now singed and smoking. Then they left, and Rodrick walked Constance home.

The following day, Rodrick awoke and turned over onto his side. On his bedside table was a shimmering rock he had found on his way home the night before. He could not help but pick it up, as it reminded him of his beloved. He picked it up and held it closer, turning back over to face the ceiling.

"Rodrick!" called out his father. "It is time to get up."

"What is the point?"

"I know that you are angry, but you will see. I did what was best for all of us."

"No, you didn't. You did what you did out of ignorance because you could not see past your own preconceived notions of what a witch is. You could not look beyond that and see her for who she really was... a sweet, kind girl who would have done anything to help others."

"That may very well be, but what she did was despicable. We would have been much better off if we had died rather than be saved through her unholy magick. At least then we would still have our souls."

At the Reid home, Constance was sitting on her sofa, still crying. Her mother walked in and sat next to her. "Have you been up all night?"

"I cannot sleep. I cannot eat. All I can think about is Phoenix. She was my best friend, and now she is gone."

"I know. Words cannot express how sorry I am. I know that you are in pain, but you have to understand where they were coming from and why this had to happen."

"No, I don't! How can you? She didn't do anything wrong!"

"Yes, she did. Witchcraft is wrong, and it's dangerous."

"How can it be wrong if it heals the land and saves people? That just doesn't make any sense!"

Her mother put her arms around her and stroked her hair, trying to comfort her. She wished she had the answers and the words to heal her daughter's broken heart, but she did not. She just hoped that someday she would understand.

Sorcha was having an equally difficult time coping, and she could not bring herself to forgive her parents for not protecting her sister. "She was your daughter!" she yelled at them. "How could you not care? How could you stand there and watch her suffer? How could you take me to watch it? Why didn't you stop them?"

"We couldn't," said her mother. "Do you have any idea how dangerous that would have been? To us… to you? You love your sister, and that is good. However, you have to understand that she betrayed us. She chose to use magick. She knew the consequences of that choice. We taught her, just as we taught you. She is no longer your sister or our daughter. She died long ago. She stopped being our daughter when she decided to partake in the devil's work. She sold her soul and sacrificed us along with her."

"How can you say that? I can't accept this. I won't. If she is no longer your daughter, then neither am I." With that, she stormed out of the house.

"Sorcha, wait!" her parents shouted. They stood and tried to go after her, but the door slammed behind them. They tried to open it, but it wouldn't budge.

"What is happening?" asked Mrs. Doyle.

"I do not know."

Suddenly, they heard screeching behind them. They turned and screamed. The last thing they ever saw was a cloud of smoke.

Wallace, Finnegan, and McCarthy were at the town hall, discussing Rodrick and Constance. "My son means well," said Finnegan. "It is not his fault that witch got her hands on him. He was a victim, just like the rest of us."

"That may be," said McCarthy. "But we need to be sure that his allegiance lies with us and with God."

Finnegan nodded, "I understand. So, what would you have me do?"

Wallace set down his water. "I think it would be best if…" Before he could finish, he began coughing, then choking.

"Wallace? Are you all right?" asked McCarthy.

However, he could not respond. His face started turning purple, and he fell to the ground. As he did, he knocked over a table, causing the lantern to topple over. It shattered and set the rug ablaze.

"Sorry, Wallace," said Finnegan as he bolted toward the door, leaving his comrade behind. McCarthy joined him. Before they could reach the door, it too slammed. The fire spread rapidly across the room. Before they even had time to react, it consumed them.

Collette and her friends were walking through the courtyard when one of them stopped short. "What is it?" asked Collette, but her friend did not answer. She simply pointed ahead. Collette turned and screamed as she saw a terrible demon standing before her.

Upon hearing the girls' screams, a man in a nearby house ran outside to check on them. "Are you all right?" he asked. "What is the matter?"

"What do you mean? The demon! The demon is the matter!"

"What demon? Where?"

"Right there, in front of us!"

"Is this another one of your delusions you spoke of?"

"Do not be ridiculous. That was never real, but he is! This demon is real, and he is going to get us. You have to stop him, please!"

"You mean to tell me you lied to the courts? None of what you said was true?"

"Do not just stand there. Please, help!"

Suddenly, the apparition roared, and the girls all screamed and fell to the ground, sobbing hysterically and crying out for help. Once again, it roared and hovered over them as if to devour them. Their hearts could no longer withstand the strain, and they gave out. There, in the streets, the four of them took their last breaths. No one knew how to respond or what had happened. Chaos ensued across the colony of Roanoke as those who betrayed Phoenix were snuffed out, one by one.

Rodrick was walking down the street near the town center when Constance caught up to him. "Rodrick, wait! Where are you going?"

"I do not know, but I…" He squinted, looking out at the street up ahead. "Is that Sorcha?"

Constance looked and saw her as well. "Yes, it is. Sorcha! What are you doing out here all alone?"

"I cannot stay home with my parents – not after what they did to Phoenix. She was my sister, their daughter… and yet they act like she meant nothing to them. They turned their backs on her, and now I am turning mine on them."

"Oh, honey. I know how much pain you are in," said Constance.

"Constance?"

"Yes, Rodrick?"

"What is happening?"

The three of them looked over toward the stake, which still stood in the center of town. Sparks were flying all around, and black smoke encircled it. Suddenly, the smoke dissipated, and a large flame burned brightly, startling them. The girls embraced each other. Rodrick stumbled backward, falling to the ground. Constance reached over to help him back up.

Suddenly, the flame went out, leaving in its place a glowing, redhaired beauty who looked down toward them. After a brief moment of stunned silence, she smiled at them and asked, "Did you miss me?"

Tabitha

By J.A. Cummings

Prudence Dunlap is hot on the trail of a witch – an ancestor who's been dead for centuries. Tabitha Dunlap was sent to the gallows, an unfortunate victim of injustice… or was she? Prudence came to Salem for answers. What she found was more than she ever expected.

"Here we are," the librarian said, bringing a leather-bound tome to her table. Prudence Dunlap sat back so she could put the book down. "Trial transcripts, Salem Village, 1690 to 1700."

"I can't believe these records still exist."

"Oh, they do. They're a little difficult to read, so if you need any help, let me know. Sometimes the ink blurs or the handwriting is poor... and spelling! Psh!" The librarian smiled behind her cat eyeglasses. "I'll just be at the circulation desk."

Prudence smiled. "Thank you!"

The librarian, Miss Peters, left Prudence alone with the precious document, a sign of trust that meant the world to her. Not every librarian so readily shared her archive.

She pulled her chestnut hair back into a ponytail, then put on her reading glasses. Her brown eyes were bright with excitement as she pulled on the archivist gloves that she brought. Prudence had worked as a genealogist for ten years, chasing down records of other people's lives from one end of the country to the other. This was the first time she had ever investigated her own family tree.

Her father had abandoned them when she was only three years old, so there were no stories she could recall. She had never met anyone on her father's side of the family, and it was only through some intense internet sleuthing that she had found her way here to Danvers, the town that had once been the center of the Salem Witch Trials in 1692.

The relative she was trailing was not one of the famous victims of that legal travesty. Tabitha Dunlap, her father's eleven-times great-grandaunt, had been executed as a witch four years after the famous Salem witch hysteria had faded and become a bad taste in everybody's mouth. Prudence hadn't even heard of the woman before last year when she'd signed onto a genealogy site and entered her father's name.

She recited the tree she knew in her head. Her father was David Dunlap, born in 1943. His father, Steven Dunlap, was a World War II veteran who had been born in 1925. Steven's father, Christian, had been a minister in Providence, Rhode Island, born in 1892. Before him had been Adrick Dunlap, born 1869; Ezekiel Dunlap, Civil War veteran, born 1841; Nathaniel Dunlap, born 1802; Edward Dunlap, born 1779; Horatio Dunlap, Revolutionary War patriot, born in 1755; Edward Dunlap I, born in 1739; Peter Dunlap, born in 1701; and Augustus Dunlap, who had lived in Salem Village in the 1690s. Tabitha had been Augustus's sister.

Such a long line of New Englanders, she thought. *Thank God the Puritans were literate and kept extensive records.*

She carefully turned the pages in the book before her. She had experience reading the handwritten records of the colonial period, which was a blessing. Prudence didn't know how someone fresh off the street would ever be able to read these pages.

It took all her self-control not to get distracted by random records. She had always loved history, especially Colonial history and the minutiae of every day. This farmer was squabbling with that squatter over unpaid rents; this farmer was suing the other for selling him a sick ram that couldn't mount his ewes. It was fascinating, and she could imagine these suits being filed today. People were the same, it seemed, no matter how many years ago they'd lived.

She finally found the records of Tabitha Dunlap's trial. On the first page, it listed her name and the name of her accuser, William White. The presiding judge was a preacher, Reverend George Davies. The names of the witnesses were also listed, and Prudence was surprised and a little saddened to see so many. It was as if the whole town had turned out to send her great-aunt to the gallows on trumped-up charges.

Prudence turned the page and saw the arrest warrant, painstakingly listing the accusations. She got out a hand-held recorder and read the words into the microphone for later transcription.

"Salem, 6th October 1696. There being complaint this day made by Mr. William White and Mr. Augustus Dunlap" – *her own brother!* – "both of Salem Village, in behalf of their Majesties for themselves and also several of their neighbors against Tabitha Dunlap, sister of the same Augustus Dunlap of Salem Village for high suspicion of sundry acts of witchcraft done or committed by her upon the bodies of Abigail Dunlap, the daughter of the same Augustus Dunlap, and Elizabeth White, wife of the same William White, both of Salem Village, whereby great hurt and damage hath been done to the bodies of said persons above named.

You are in their Majesties' names hereby required to apprehend and bring before us Tabitha Dunlap of Salem Village on Monday morning next, being the thirteenth day of this October, at approximately eleven of the clock, at the public meeting house in the town, for examination relating to the premises above stated.

To Jacob Pittman, Marshall of the County of Essex."

She turned off the recorder.

Wow. Her own brother turned her in, and she supposedly did something to her niece and this William White's wife? Prudence pursed her lips. It seemed that someone had taken to the law to resolve a family drama. She wondered if there was an inheritance involved.

The next page was a first-hand account by Jacob Pittman, relating the happenings when he tried to arrest Tabitha. Prudence read the most fantastical description she had ever seen in a legal document, open-mouthed in amazement. According to Pittman's account, when he arrived at the house where Tabitha lived, she was in the process of skinning some poor animal and muttering words in a "foreign tongue" over the hapless beast.

When he told her why he was there, Tabitha flung the beast at him and climbed the outside of the wall of her house, trying to escape over the roof. His deputies climbed after her, and one claimed that she had "spat fire from her mouth" and burned him in the face. They managed to capture her using ropes and an iron fireplace poker from her own house.

Sounds like she put up a fight. But spitting fire? Really? Prudence chuckled. *What was she, some sort of dragon?*

The transcripts became even more far-fetched the longer she read. Tabitha attacked the judge's wife in her dreams, causing her to miscarry. She levitated in the courtroom and called on Satan to defend her. She made her accusers crawl on the floor and bark like dogs with a single command, and she made all the milk in the village turn sour.

It was astonishing to Prudence that supposedly knowledgeable and educated adults believed the sort of things that she was reading.

Tabitha had been found guilty of her supposed crimes and was hanged that very afternoon, which was a departure. Normally, they kept their condemned witches in the dungeon of the sheriff's house for months until they got around to killing them. Apparently, they had been eager to be rid of Tabitha.

Prudence sat back and considered the story before her. She hadn't seen any description of what her relative had supposedly done to her victims, and the pandemonium in the courtroom during her trial was too extreme to be believed. She knew that the people in Salem had suffered from ergot poisoning, a sort of madness caused by mold on the grains that they used to make their bread. That was the only thing that could have possibly explained anyone believing the nonsense she had just read.

If she followed the pattern of the victims of the earlier Salem witch trials, Tabitha had probably been a spinster with a sharp tongue and an attitude problem. She was probably prickly and unpleasant, and she might even have abandoned the Puritan faith. Prudence imagined a fiercely independent woman who didn't want or need a man and who lived her life on her own terms – a dangerous thing to be in the Puritan colony of Massachusetts. Prudence thought her ancestress might have been the Colonial equivalent of a suffragette, and she had been handled just as roughly.

The last page of the document detailed how she had been taken to the hanging tree on the outskirts of town, where she was hanged by the neck until dead. Death took twenty minutes to come to her. Prudence rubbed her own throat in sympathy, imagining how awful a slow, strangling demise like that must have been and how much suffering poor Tabitha had endured. It was an awful story. The worst part was the end. As a condemned witch, she was denied a proper Christian burial in the Salem Village cemetery, and her body had been cut down and tossed into the woods to be devoured by animals.

The unfairness of the entire story made Prudence burn. She had read similar tales in other families' histories, but the knowledge that she shared blood with a woman who had suffered and died so cruelly made it all so much more personal. Her heart was heavy as she closed the book and stripped away her white gloves.

She went to the circulation desk and found Miss Peters. "I've finished the book," she told her. "I was wondering… could you tell me where the hanging tree was located?"

"Well, it's long gone now, of course," the librarian said. "But there's a marker where it used to be. It's just a short walk away, on the edge of the forest."

"The forest where they threw the bodies… has it been developed?"

"Oh, no. Nobody would ever build there," she said, chuckling. "Many people won't even walk there. They say it's haunted."

Prudence sighed. "Well, if any forest had reason to have ghosts, that would be it. Thank you."

"Not a problem. If you need any other documents, just let me know."

"I will. Um… Could you give me directions?"

Miss Peters did one better and drew a map on a piece of paper from the printer. Prudence thanked her and left the library. She was still sad, mourning a relative she had never known. Tabitha had been falsely accused, convicted in a sham trial, and put to a horrific death – all for no reason. It was a travesty, and she felt very sorry for Tabitha.

The map was easy to follow, and Prudence found herself on the edge of a stand of elms, maples, and oaks. The marker for the hanging tree was solemn, as it should have been, and she wished she had brought flowers. It was the only grave marker Tabitha would ever have.

Even though the sun was high in the sky, the forest was dark and foreboding. She hesitated on the edge, her hand on the bole of a dying elm. She didn't know what she was afraid of. Maybe she was just bothered by the knowledge that people's corpses had been thrown in there without ceremony or care. Prudence took a deep breath, screwed up her courage, and stepped in.

The footing was treacherous, with many fallen limbs and rocks underfoot. Prudence walked carefully, holding the trees with her hands for balance. Ahead of her, she could see a place where the land sloped down sharply to form a ravine of sorts. This was probably where they threw the bodies.

The wind through the trees made a low, moaning sound, and it was easy to imagine that she was hearing the plaintive cries of the people who had been disposed of in this place. The breeze was cold and getting increasingly blustery, and her ears were hurting from the unseasonable cold. She wished she had her winter coat.

There was a distant rumble, and she looked up at the sky for signs of rain. The sound wasn't thunder. The ground beneath her feet suddenly gave way, sending her skidding down into the ravine. Prudence scrambled for handholds, but she was falling too quickly, and all the branches she grabbed broke loose or bent in her hands. She screeched in fear as she tumbled, narrowly missing a stout oak, rolling head over feet down to the bottom.

When she finally stopped falling, she lay for a moment to catch her breath. She wasn't hurt, apart from some bumps and bruises. She slowly sat up.

The ground gave way beneath her again, and she fell straight down into the darkness. Prudence landed hard on rocks and rubble, knocking the wind out of her. There was almost no light in the hole she had fallen into, and drooping roots from the vegetation above her tickled her face. She batted them away and tried to stand. There was no even ground, though, and she put her hands out, struggling to pull herself up onto all fours.

Her eyes adjusted to the darkness, and she realized that she had come face-to-face with a skull.

Prudence cried out in surprise and jumped back. The skull was connected to a skeleton, which still had some tattered remnants of black cloth around it. A rope was tied in a noose around the dead person's neck, and the wrists were bound in iron manacles. She stared in disbelief.

It's one of them. One of the condemned, she thought. *My God... still bound and with the noose? That's horrible! Barbaric!*

She burned with anger for the unfortunate soul in the hole with her, and she resolved that she would get a proper burial for this person, or at least finally release them from the iron bonds.

She used the roots of the trees around the hole to help her climb back out. Once she was on solid ground again, she reached into her cross-body purse, which had somehow stayed with her through her acrobatic trip through the terrain. She grabbed her phone and dialed 9-1-1.

"911. What is your emergency?"

"I've just found a dead body."

****

The police came quickly. A young sheriff met her at the hanging tree marker.

"Miss Dunlap?" he asked.

"Yes."

"Sheriff James Pittman." He offered her his hand, and she accepted the handshake. His grip was firm but not crushing. "Tell me what happened."

"I was walking in the woods and fell," she answered. "I ended up in a hole, and there was a body at the bottom."

"A body?"

"Well, a skeleton."

Pittman frowned. "Can you show me where?"

She led him to the hole, and he whistled when he saw what she had discovered.

"I wasn't expecting to come face-to-face with a witch today," he admitted, "but I'm glad it's not someone fresher, if you know what I mean."

Prudence nodded. "I do."

"I think this is more a case for the archaeologists than for our homicide detectives."

The two of them went back to the sheriff's vehicle, and he placed a call to Danvers College. A team from the university came quickly and set up an archaeological site, complete with cordons and sharpened trowels. They let Prudence stay and watch while they worked.

They photographed the body where it lay in the ravine, then carefully took the skeleton out of the hole, piece by piece. They treated the dead person with much more respect than his or her contemporaries had, and Prudence was pleased when the manacles fell away as the archaeologists picked up the arm bones. When the shackles slid off the bones, a rush of hot wind blew past her; it sounded almost like a sigh of relief.

When the archaeologists had gone, taking the skeleton and the manacles with them, the sheriff was still at the scene. He moved slowly around the hole, looking closely at the ground. Prudence walked over to him.

"Looking for more bodies?"

He smiled. "Yeah, I guess I am. They hanged about fifty people here over the years, and those bodies all got tossed in here. I think a lot of families snuck in during the night to get their loved ones and give them proper burials, but you never know. There might be more out here."

"Fifty witches?" she asked. "That's a lot more than I thought there were."

"People only think about the 1692 episode," he told her, straightening. He put his hands on his hips and looked around. The wind caught his brown hair and lifted it from his forehead, and his blue eyes had a distant look. "They don't talk about the onesie-twosie hangings."

She looked at the name on his breast pocket. "Pittman. Any relation to Marshall Jacob Pittman?"

The sheriff grimaced. "Yeah. Great-great-however-many-times-great grandfather." He smiled at her. "He's sort of an embarrassment, but it's cool to have a connection to the history around here."

"Why is he an embarrassment?"

"Would you be proud of an ancestor who arrested and hanged people for witchcraft when it doesn't exist?"

Prudence smiled. It existed as a religion, but it certainly wasn't the outrageous thing that the accusers claimed. "Well... no."

"Didn't think so." He gestured toward his car. "Do you need a ride anywhere?"

"No, I'm fine. My car is at the library. I was doing some research and thought I'd come out here to see where they dumped the bodies. I certainly didn't expect to find one."

The sheriff chuckled. "Made for an exciting day, I'm sure."

She glanced down at her mud-stained jeans and sighed. "Yeah, exciting isn't quite the word I'd use, but I guess it works."

"I'll be going, then. Thank you for calling, and good luck with your research."

They shook hands at his car and parted ways.

****

By dinner time, the bruises were making themselves known, and Prudence was painfully aware that she had, in fact, jammed a finger and a shoulder and seriously banged her knee on something. She took a long bath, grateful that her inner hedonist had inspired her to get a jacuzzi room at the hotel. She took an over-the-counter muscle relaxer and washed it down with half a bottle of red wine, which left her limp as a noodle when she finally fell into bed.

She had a vivid dream, probably a combination of the day's immersion in history and the combination of substances she had swallowed. In the dream, she was walking through Salem Village during the 1690s. A woman with dark hair and eyes walked beside her. The woman was taking her on a tour of the little village, and Prudence just knew that it was Tabitha.

"That is Master White's house," Tabitha said. "He keeps a black woman as a slave and takes her to his bed when his wife takes ill. Lately, he's been asking me to make his wife ill a lot... and so I do. He pays me for the privilege. I suppose he prefers his slave's embrace to his wife's, but having seen her, I do not fault him for his choice, pale and useless creature that she is."

Prudence saw the sheriff from the forest. "He shouldn't be here. He's modern."

The other woman clicked her tongue. "That's Jacob Pittman. Their Majesties' witch catcher. Mind him well, my dear."

She took Prudence to a small shop. "This business," she said. "My brother claims it and half the earnings, but he does none of the labor. I sell tea here and herbs for cooking, and when someone comes to me and asks just right, I sell them potions to ease their pains or free them of the babes they have no wish to bear. I'm just a woman helping other women, but my brother wants this shop to give it as his daughter's dowry."

"That's why you hurt his daughter," Prudence said.

"Hurt her?" Tabitha laughed. "I poisoned her, my dear. The only problem is that the little monster lived. I didn't make the potion strong enough."

"They're going to come for you," she warned.

Tabitha looked at her as if she'd gone mad. "They already have, my dear. I'm quite dead."

Her face melted into a grinning skull, and a noose appeared around her neck. She raised her hands, and they were bound by iron shackles.

"You found my body today." The smell of death was all around, and it was making Prudence ill. Tabitha morphed back into her living self and smiled. "Thank you for that. I'm in your debt, but now I need your help with something else."

"What?" she asked, afraid. The sun that had been shining outside was gone now, and they were standing in the shop in the dark of night.

Tabitha lit a candle with flint and steel. "I need to be avenged. All the souls who participated in my trial are reborn, and with your arrival, they all have come together in this town. White. My brother." She spat the word. "His wife. His slave. The judge. They're all here, ready to be punished for what they did to me. Can I trust you to do this?"

Prudence balked. "I'm not a vengeful person, and..."

"You would deny me peace? I cannot rest until these people are punished."

"These people didn't do anything. It was their ancestors."

"No!" Tabitha slapped a table with her hand, and the sound was like a clap of thunder. "They are the same souls. They still wear this sin around their necks like this noose!"

She transformed again, this time into her death state. The noose appeared, stretched taut above her head. Her face was discolored, and her tongue was swollen and extended between her lips. Her bloodshot eyes protruded from the sockets. She made a horrible gagging, choking sound, and Prudence put her hands over her ears.

"Stop it!"

The cry ripped from her throat in the quiet of her hotel room, and she found herself sitting bolt upright in bed. The bedside clock told her that it was already morning, although she felt like she hadn't slept at all. Prudence rose from the bed and found that she could barely walk, still under the influence of the alcohol she had consumed. She found her phone and dialed a pre-programmed number.

Almost immediately, her mother answered. "Hello?"

"Hi, Mom."

"Sweetheart! How is Salem?"

"It's… kind of amazing. I found the trial transcript for Tabitha's trial, and then I went walking in the woods, and…"

Her mother's voice was careful. It was always dangerous when her mother sounded careful. "And?"

"And I think I found Tabitha."

She told her about the landslide and the fall and about the body at the bottom of the ravine. Her mother listened attentively, then asked, "How do you know it was Tabitha? It could have been any of the victims of the witch hunts."

Prudence put her face in her hand. "Because she came to me in a dream and told me so."

There was stunned silence on the other end of the call. "Explain."

In a halting voice, she told her mother about the dream and the exhortation toward revenge. She was more unsettled than she should have been from a simple dream, and her hands wouldn't stop shaking.

"It's crazy, though, right?" she asked after she was done relaying the story. "Dead people can't come to talk to the living in dreams, and the chances that was actually her are astronomical. I mean... please tell me it's crazy."

There was a long silence, then her mother said, "I can't."

"Why not?" She pulled her knees up toward her chest. "Mom..."

She sighed. "There's a lot I haven't told you, but it looks like it's time you knew. I'm coming down to meet you. I've got to take care of some things here, but I'll be there in Danvers tomorrow at around lunchtime. Then we can talk."

Prudence frowned, feeling like a frightened child. "Mom, you're scaring me."

"I'm sorry, baby. I'll explain everything when I get there. Just hold tight. I'll meet you at your hotel."

She nodded, even though she knew her mother couldn't see her. "Okay, Mom. I'll see you then."

They ended the call, and Prudence stared at the phone for a long time.

She ended up falling asleep again and stayed in bed until almost two in the afternoon, the latest she'd slept in since her college days. Prudence took her time showering, amazed by the purple bruises that stood out all along her legs and on her back. She had fallen farther and hit the ground harder than she'd realized.

She decided to go back to the library. This time, she wanted to find a map of the original village so she could compare it to the one that she had seen in her dream. She wasn't certain if she wanted the two villages to match or to be nothing alike.

There was another researcher there when she arrived. He was gorgeous, and she had a hard time not staring at him. He had sun-bleached streaks in his blond hair and an amazingly fit body. He looked like he should have been a model, not someone stuck in a library looking at old records.

By happenstance, the book she needed to look at was near the table where he was sitting, and he glanced up when she walked by. He smiled, and she smiled back and saw that his eyes were the bluest she had ever seen. She tried to seem calm and collected as she hunted for the right book, but she could feel him watching her.

The book she needed wasn't in its place, so she sighed.

"Everything okay?" the man asked.

Prudence turned around to smile at him. "Yeah, I just can't find the book I was looking for."

He grinned sheepishly. "That's because I have it." He motioned to a stack of books on the table before him. "I'll let you use it if you have dinner with me tonight."

She raised her eyebrows. "That, sir, is blackmail."

"Why, yes. Yes, it is." He tilted his head. "Is it working?"

"Like a charm." She offered her hand. "Prudence Dunlap."

"John Campbell."

She sat down across the table from him. "Do I get to see the book now, or only after I pay up?"

He laughed. "Now."

John slid the book toward her, his hands in archivist gloves. She took her own pair out of her bag and pulled them on. "Nice to know that you're responsible with these old pages," she told him.

"Well, I'm a history professor, so I'd better be."

"Oh! Do you teach at Danvers College?"

"Sure do." He watched her as she carefully opened the book. "You wouldn't happen to be the same Prudence Dunlap who found the body in the woods, would you?"

"Wow. Good news travels fast."

"Especially in small towns like this." She turned a few more pages, and he said, "You know, with a name like Prudence Dunlap, I feel like you should be in that book, not reading it."

She smiled. "My ancestors are in this book, so I guess it's a compromise."

"Mine are, too."

She didn't recall seeing the name Campbell in any of the documents, and as far as she knew, the Highland Scots hadn't started leaving their country yet in the 1690s. "Who are your ancestors?"

"I'm actually descended from William White."

He sounded embarrassed, and she looked up at him. "Wow."

"What wow?'

"Your grandpa sent my grandaunt to the gallows."

"Er… yeah. Sorry."

Prudence laughed and shook her head. "I'm not personally offended, but I have it on good authority that she's pissed."

John chuckled. "I would be, too."

"Well, of course… I still can't believe they ever executed people on charges of witchcraft. I mean, there's witchcraft today, but it's not like they thought back then, and anyway, nobody then knew anything about it. Everybody they killed was totally innocent."

"Not exactly true," John said hesitantly. "I'm not trying to mansplain here, but…"

She sat back. "Oh, by all means. Go ahead. You're the actual expert here, so it's not mansplaining."

John took a breath. "Okay, here's the thing. In my family, we've got stories that have been repeated about William White and about Tabitha Dunlap."

Prudence crossed her arms and sat back. "This should be interesting."

"It is. I don't know how true it is, but… the family story is that William White had a slave woman that he wanted to have as a mistress. He couldn't sleep with her when his wife was well, so he had Tabitha Dunlap make potions to make his wife sick. Then while she was recuperating and in isolation or quarantine or whatever, he would be with his slave."

Prudence went cold. The story he was telling was exactly what the Tabitha figure in her dream had told her. She stared at him wordlessly, stunned.

He shrugged one shoulder. "Of course, I'm sure neither his wife nor his slave was happy about the arrangement, but at the time…"

"Yeah. Men could do anything they wanted to do at the time. But Tabitha was just doing what he hired her to do. That's no reason to turn her in and accuse her of witchcraft."

"The accusation wasn't about the potions. It was about what she did after he decided to stop paying for them."

She was intrigued. "What happened?"

"William went to her house one night and told her that he wasn't going to be paying for the potions anymore. She depended on that income to survive, so she saw him ending their business as a real threat, which I suppose it was. She tried to convince him to keep buying them, but he wouldn't have it. He left that night, supposedly vowing to turn over a new leaf."

"Unlikely," Prudence judged.

"Yeah. Well, she went ballistic. That night, he woke up to her hovering over his bed, choking him."

"How did she get in?"

"That's the thing," John said. "According to the story, she wasn't physically there. She was just sort of... suspended in the air over his bed with her hands wrapped around his throat."

Prudence laughed. "He was dreaming."

"You'd think, but he had handprints on his neck the next morning. From then on, it was like an invisible abuser had moved into the house. His daughter was slapped, punched, kicked, stabbed with needles, and even thrown down a flight of stairs – all by someone nobody could see. And whenever it happened, they swore they could hear Tabitha laughing."

"No way."

"I know. It sounds crazy, but my granddad, the one who told this story, swears that it's true."

She shook her head. She wanted to disbelieve the story, but she couldn't, especially given the things she'd heard in her dream the previous night. Prudence whispered, "Go on."

"Believe it or not, it gets weirder." He leaned forward. "From that night forward, everything went wrong. His horse dropped dead when it had been perfectly healthy just moments before. His wife died. His slave died. His daughter's fiancé backed out of the marriage and left her high and dry. His chickens died; his crops failed... he was falling into ruin."

"And that's when he accused her?"

"Yeah." He sighed. "Supposedly, everything started going right again as soon as she was dead."

They were silent for a minute, probably to the delight of the librarian. Prudence finally said, "Wow. That is the biggest pile of bullshit I have ever heard."

John broke into a smile. "Right? My older relatives swear it's all one-hundred percent true, though."

She struggled to find some plausible deniability. "That arrangement with the potions and your ancestor wanting to be with his slave... was that ever written down anywhere?"

"No. To my knowledge, it's just family fable."

"I must have seen it someplace, though."

"Why do you say that?"

"Because..." She weighed the merits of telling him the truth, and she decided that since she probably would never see him again, it didn't matter if he thought that she was crazy. "Because I dreamed that Tabitha came to me last night and told me that same story."

John stared at her, and she regretted opening her mouth. After a long minute, he said, "Wow. Seriously?"

"Well, yeah. I'm not going to lie about my dreams. Why would I?"

"That's crazy."

"Don't I know it." She sighed. "Anyway, just forget I said anything. This whole conversation is turning strange. I, uh… I'm going to look at the book now."

They fell silent, each returning to their research. She found the map she was looking for, and to her creeping horror, it matched her dream exactly. She shook her head.

"This is impossible."

"What is?"

"This. This village map… it's exactly the way I saw Salem in my dream last night."

He looked up at her. "Have you studied Salem for long?'

"No, not really. Not so that I'd have the map in my head."

"Maybe you saw it before."

She was unconvinced. "Maybe… I appreciate you trying to un-weird this for me."

John closed the book he was looking at and smiled at her. "Would you like to make it lunch instead of dinner? Get a little space from here for a minute?"

Prudence thought for a moment, then nodded. "Yeah. Just let me sketch this first."

"No need. I have a copy in my car." She raised an eyebrow at him, and he explained, "History professor, living in the middle of where significant history happened. I've got a lot of research and reference materials."

She let him lead her out to his car, which was a new foreign job that was immaculately clean on the outside. The backseat was covered in bankers' boxes filled with papers and stacks of books, which gave credence to his claims of being a professor.

He opened the passenger door for her. "Miss Dunlap? Your chariot."

Prudence chuckled and got in. "You're weird."

"I know," he admitted with a light sigh as he settled in behind the steering wheel. "All the best people are."

He took her to a casual dining restaurant, where they were seated at a table by a window. In the sunlight, he looked like Hollywood's idea of a surfer, and she found herself staring at him while he chatted. She was powerfully drawn to him, something she hadn't felt for a very long time.

She was so entranced that she failed to notice when he stopped talking. She blinked. "I'm so sorry... What were you saying?"

"Nothing interesting, apparently," he said, smiling.

She blushed. "I'm sorry. I'm just... distracted."

He looked into her eyes. "By me?"

She felt her face heat, but she decided to be brave and tell the truth. "Yes."

John's smile widened. "That's quite a compliment. Thank you."

"I'm so sorry. I'm normally not like this, but..."

"It's okay. Sometimes things happen." The look he gave her was intense and burned into her, sending shockwaves of desire through her body. "Sometimes we need to let them happen."

"I..."

She was interrupted by the arrival of the waitress with their bill. John put down his credit card and studied her face.

She was certain that her need for him was plain to see, and she didn't know if that was good or bad.

"Would you like to go back to my place?"

Prudence half-expected him to ask her to see his reference materials as a pretext, but it seemed that he was too honest for that. She could only nod.

When they reached his house, John took her by the hand and led her inside. He closed the door and turned the lock. She was nervous and excited, and her desire for him was raging. When he turned to face her, she could see that he was feeling the same.

John took her face in his hands and kissed her passionately. She responded in kind, opening her mouth so he could spear his tongue inside. Prudence wrapped her arms around him and pulled him closer, pressing their bodies together. He groaned in the back of his throat, then bent and picked her up in his strong arms. Still kissing her, he carried her into the bedroom.

****

They fell asleep in the afterglow as the afternoon faded into evening. Prudence felt happy and warm. She was lying on her side, facing the edge of the bed. John had been spooning her, but he had rolled away in his sleep.

The sound of choking woke her, and Prudence turned to John in alarm. His eyes were bulging, and he was clawing at his throat as if he was trying to pull something away. As Prudence watched, a noose appeared around his neck, pulling tighter and tighter. At the end of the rope, she saw

Tabitha. She was standing at the end of the bed with a maniacal grin on her face.

"Stop it!" she shouted.

John's hands went through the spectral rope when he tried to grab it to pull it loose, but when Prudence tried, she closed her hand around solid hemp. She yanked the rope out of Tabitha's hands, and with a snarl, the ghost disappeared.

Prudence quickly took the noose off John's neck. He coughed and gagged, gasping for air. There were rope burns on his neck.

"Oh, my God," he finally said. "What the hell was that?"

She embraced him, and he clung to her in his fear. "Tabitha."

It took time for them to calm down. They showered and dressed, almost afraid to speak. They sat in the living room on his couch, his arm around her shoulders, her head on his chest. She finally broke the silence. "Are you okay?"

"Yeah, more or less." He took a deep breath. "I don't even know how to process this. I just... How do you cope with this? I was just attacked by a dead witch."

"I don't know. I've never experienced anything like this before."

"How did you know it was Tabitha?"

She straightened. "I saw her in a dream. She was walking me through Salem Village and asking me to help her get revenge on the people who killed her."

He raised an eyebrow. "How are you supposed to get revenge on people who are already dead?"

"In the dream, she said that all of their souls had been reborn and that they were all here in Danvers right now." She shook her head. "It sounds so insane."

"It's not. Not really."

"Thank you for not thinking I'm crazy."

He smiled ruefully. "Crazy doesn't leave rope burns."

They stayed together that night in her hotel room. There were no more appearances by Tabitha's vengeful ghost, but they both had nightmares about what had transpired. Tired and listless, they went to breakfast.

"I was thinking," John told her. "I think I know someone who can help."

"Who?"

"He's a friend of mine, Tom Smith. He's the reverend of a Spiritualist church here in town, and he's also a ghost hunter. He probably would have some idea of what we should do."

She sighed and stirred her tea. "Any help would be great because I am completely out of my element here."

"Yeah… Me, too."

When they were finished with their meal, he called ahead and told his friend what had happened. Smith invited them to come to his house, and John drove them there.

Tom Smith was a haggard-looking man whose relative youth was undercut by the look in his eyes. He greeted them at the door.

"John," he said, giving his friend a hug. "Those burns look terrible. Come in."

"Thanks. They feel terrible. Tom, this is Prudence. Prudence, Tom Smith."

She shook his hand. "Nice to meet you."

"Likewise." He brought them into his cluttered living room. "Please, have a seat. Since we're talking about the witch trials, I should tell you that I'm descended from Reverend Davies."

"The judge who condemned Tabitha," Prudence identified.

"Yes."

"Then you're in danger, too," John said.

"Most likely. It would certainly explain the last few nights." He pulled down his shirt collar to reveal livid scratches on his skin. "I've been having visitations, too."

"Jesus," John swore.

"I took the liberty of calling a colleague of mine, a witchcraft specialist and demonologist. It just so happens that she's going to be arriving in Danvers today. She was already on the road when I called her."

"Who is it?" John asked.

"Millicent Dunlap."

Prudence gasped. "My mother?!"

Tom nodded. "I have a feeling that she's got some things she needs to tell you. Where were you going to meet her?"

"At the hotel," she said. Her head was spinning. "I... This is too much."

"We should meet her together," John said. "Get everyone on the same page."

"I agree." Tom stood up. "I can drive."

Millicent called from the lobby, and Prudence brought her up to her room, where Tom and John were waiting.

"This is John Campbell," Prudence told her mother. "I guess I don't need to introduce Tom Smith."

"No, you don't." She shook John's hand and gave Tom a quick embrace before she sat on the edge of the bed. Prudence sat down in the desk chair, and the men occupied the chairs by the little table. "First of all, Pru, I owe you an apology. I've been keeping things from you."

She felt a rush of anger. "No kidding."

Millicent sighed. "I was hoping to protect you from this. You see, witchcraft is a family tradition, and Tabitha isn't just a distant relative of your father's – she's also my ancestor." She waited for the news to sink in. "We have been practicing witches for generations. Tabitha wasn't the first to have powers, but she was the first to misuse them. After she was executed, the rest of the family ran to Providence, where we have remained to this day."

"You never told me."

"It's a terrible burden that I wanted to spare you. The more you know about the Shadow World, the more the Shadow World knows you. It can be dangerous."

John said, "Well, Tabitha knows us all pretty well, apparently, and she's got one hell of a grudge. How do we stop her before she kills us all?"

"You take her bones back to where they were found, and then you salt and burn them."

Prudence gaped at her mother in shock. "What? Are you serious?"

Her mother nodded. "It's the only way. Where is the body now?"

"In the archaeology lab at Danvers College," she answered.

"Behind locked doors, no doubt," Millicent mused.

Tom smiled. "Luckily, we know a professor who has the keys."

John nodded. "Once the school closes for the night, I can get the body."

"See that you do," Millicent told him, "and be careful to bring everything – every bone, every hair. She needs to be complete for this to work."

"And if she's burned when she's not complete?" Tom asked.

She answered solemnly, "Disaster."

****

After midnight, John and Prudence crept into the building that held the history professors' offices as well as the archaeology lab. He unlocked the lab and turned on the light.

The body was laid out on a metal table, the bones placed in their correct anatomical positions. Prudence was almost surprised the skeleton didn't rise up to attack them.

"Can you see a bag or a box or anything we can use?" he asked.

She looked around and found a box full of printer paper under a desk. She emptied out the reams and brought the box to the table.

"I think this will hold it."

"Yeah. Perfect."

She couldn't bring herself to touch the bones, but John quickly gathered them up and put them in the box. They were careful to collect every piece of bone from the table, leaving nothing behind. He held the box.

"I'll carry this gross thing," he told her. "You drive."

They hurried out of the building with their contraband, watching to be certain none of the campus security guards were around. She slid in behind the wheel while he sat in the passenger seat, the box of Tabitha's remains in his lap. He gave her directions, and she drove them to the hanging tree marker. Millicent and Tom were waiting for them when they arrived.

He had flashlights and a rope in the trunk, and she collected them along with the box of Kosher sea salt they'd bought at the grocery store. She passed out the flashlights, and the group made their way into the forest.

The woods seemed to be alive, determined to stop their progress. The tree branches reached out and grabbed at Prudence's hair and clothes, and the ground felt weak and unsteady. She was afraid that the bottom would fall out again, and that she'd tumble like she did before.

It took them a long while to make their way safely down the incline to the cave she had discovered, but they finally reached it. The beams from the flashlights illuminated the inside of the hole, and John handed the box of bones to Tom.

"I'm going to jump down in there. Hand the box to me once I'm down. I don't want to take the chance of dropping anything."

He tied the rope to a nearby tree and dropped the other end into the hole. He tugged to make sure the knot was secure, then lowered himself into the darkness. Prudence shone her flashlight down the hole for him, trying to help him see where he was going.

John made sure his footing was secure, then turned and held his hands up for the box. Tom carefully handed it to him.

"Do you want anybody else to come down there?" Prudence asked.

"No. There's barely enough room for me and Tabitha," he said.

He put the box of bones on the ground and held up his hand again. Prudence put the box of salt in his palm, and he poured it over the bones.

Millicent leaned down. "Get out of the hole before you start the fire," she warned. "We're going to use lighter fluid to make sure it burns."

"Blessed lighter fluid?" Tom asked.

"Of course."

John climbed back out. He stood beside Prudence and brushed off his hands. "Well, here comes the fun part."

In the distance, a howl split the night air. It was human and animal at the same time, and wholly chilling. Millicent looked over her shoulder.

"Quickly. She'll try to stop us."

She took the lighter fluid and squirted it over the box, soaking the cardboard and the bones and salt that it contained. Prudence struck a match and dropped it in.

The hole filled with a bright red flame, burning hotter than any oven. Greenish smoke rose from the bones, and the trees around them began to shake. Tabitha emerged from the smoke, floating a foot off the ground, shrieking with rage.

She flew at Tom, her fingers aiming for his face. Prudence pushed Tom out of the way. Tabitha changed course and headed for Prudence, her teeth grinding.

"*Spiritus immunda erit abeirunt!*" Millicent shouted. "Begone, unclean spirit!"

Tabitha stopped short, immobilized by the words her descendant shouted. She snarled and turned to face Millicent. Her spectral body began to smolder, red flames dancing along her dress and hair. She screamed and tried to beat out the flames, but they would not go out. She twisted and turned, writhing in the fire.

Millicent inscribed a sigil in the air with her finger, leaving a contrail of blue light. "*Ab inferno redire!*" she commanded. "Go back to the hell you came from!"

Tabitha shrieked and shook. Her specter vibrated and shook like an old movie reel that was out of sync. Holes rimmed with red flame appeared in her form, and the noose and shackles reappeared. She threw her head back and roared in pain and rage.

"Go!"

She exploded in a rush of hot air that smelled of death. The flames in the hole lost their red color but continued to burn.

Prudence looked at her mother. "Is it over?"

"It's over."

They stood over the hole until the fire burned itself out, leaving nothing but a pile of ash behind. The sunrise bathed the wood in gold, and a peaceful feeling descended over them. Prudence hugged John, and Tom and Millicent shared a knowing look.

"This was the weirdest experience of my life," Prudence said.

"Mine, too."

"Wait for it." Millicent shook her head. "The Shadow World knows about you now."

John looked at her calmly. "Well, we know about it, too."

"You have a lot to learn."

Prudence looked at her mother with new eyes. "Maybe you can teach us."

She smiled. "Guaranteed."

They turned to walk back to the car, leaving the forest behind.

The End

The Summoning
Lindy S. Hudis

The terror begins as a group of Satanic pagans tries to call forth a malevolent demon from the dark depths of hell, a spirit known in this world as Bloody Mary, the "Mirror Witch."

New England. The 1600s.

It was late, just after midnight. The dark, New England sky was briefly illuminated by a flash of lightning, the roar of thunder not too far behind. Water splashed pedestrians as buggies hurriedly made their way through the driving rain.

Father Connelly, an elderly priest, struggled to make his way through the thick brush and bramble. He stumbled, grabbing a tree to catch his fall before resting his frail body against the trunk. His frightened and careworn face looked off into the distance.

Lightning struck behind an eerie-looking cabin in the woods. The priest felt the powerful, supernatural presence being disturbed and summoned into the world as he spied with horror the shadowy figures through the window, a strange aura growing in intensity around the dilapidated building.

He checked his pocket, pulling out a Bible and turning the pages until he found the Lord's Prayer. "Our Father who art in heaven, hallowed be thy name. Thy kingdom come; thy will be done on earth as it is in heaven…" He tucked the Bible safely back into his pocket, steeled himself, and pressed on. "Give us this day our daily bread and forgive us our trespasses, as we forgive those who trespass against us…"

A group of five encircled a large pentagram on the floor of the cabin, one at each point of the star. They were sitting cross-legged, bending from the waist, eyes rolled back in their heads as they repeated an incantation in a monotone.

The leader read from a large book of ancient spells in his lap. He had a distinctive tattoo on his lower, inner left forearm, just above the wrist.

The pagans began to chant, "Nans lum bek hans ba sha… Nans lum bek hans ba sha…"

Above the fireplace, there was a mirror, which started to bend and morph strangely. Another bolt of lightning flashed, revealing a faint, ghostly visage in the window.

Father Connelly, out of breath and on the verge of collapsing, approached the entrance.

"Lead us not into temptation but deliver us from evil. For thine is the Kingdom, the Power, and the Glory forever. Amen." He continued to pray as he reached the front door; sparks of light began to engulf the tiny home, pushing him back down the path. He rose to his feet and pressed on. "The Lord is my shepherd; I shall not want. He maketh me to lie down in green pastures, and leadeth me beside the still waters…"

The group increased the speed and intensity of the chant. The fireplace roared, and the mirror bent almost to the breaking point. The priest struggled to reach the door, then leaned against it.

"He restoreth my soul; He leadeth me in the path of righteousness for His name's sake." The priest hauled back and plowed into the door with all his might. The door gave way, and the priest came charging into the room. He headed right for the group leader and large book, but a force from the mirror pulled him back toward the fireplace, trying to drag him into the hearth.

The broken door swayed violently back and forth on its one remaining hinge, the elements invading the tiny space.

"…Yea, though I walk through the valley of the shadow of death, I shall fear no evil, for thou art with me."

Without panicking and with serene confidence, the priest gradually started to break free, dragging himself along the floor, his nails digging into the wood, bleeding and tearing. He was pulled back a few times, but he continued to resist the evil force with the power of his faith.

"Thy rod and thy staff, they comfort me. Thou preparest a table before me in the presence of mine enemies…

The group leader surreptitiously tore a page out of the book and slipped it into his pocket. The group continued chanting throughout.

"…Thou anointest my head with oil; my cup runneth over…"

The priest, his tunic partly ablaze, broke free and threw himself toward the leader. His Bible fell to the floor and was immediately sucked back into the fire, which momentarily burst with a brilliant, pure white light. They struggled over the book, but the priest finally wrestled it from the hands of the leader, who scurried away out the door.

The mirror visage emitted a blood-curdling scream, the surface pulsated and glowed viciously, and the fireplace became an inferno as the priest turned toward the evil apparition, raising the book above his head as his lower body and legs ignited.

"Surely, goodness and mercy shall follow me all the days of my life…"

The group leader stopped and looked back toward the cabin. The cabin glowed wickedly, enhanced by lightning flashes, fire raging within; chanting and howling are faintly heard.

The pagan leader pulled out the page from his pocket. A blast of fire shot out of a stone pit. A smoky, angry face sneered and snarled as fiery tentacles reached out to him, but he reeled back and ran off through the forest, clutching the torn-out page. The apparition was gone as suddenly as it appeared, a slight wisp of smoke following the fiery spiral back into the pit.

The priest held the book over his head.

"…And I will dwell in the house of The Lord forever. Amen."

The group suddenly stopped chanting. One of them attacked the priest as the others charged for the door, which suddenly and violently slammed back into place in the frame, the wood bowing outward, creaking and cracking. They scrambled for the high window, climbing over each other as they struggled to get out; one of them made it halfway out.

The priest knocked the attacker away with the large book, then hurled it into the fire. The fire erupted explosively, engulfing the room and its trapped occupants in flames. The one struggling in the window screamed in agony as his legs ignited; suddenly, he was yanked back by another man, fully engulfed, who started to climb out but was overcome and collapsed back into the room.

The priest crossed himself, then placed his hands together in a final, silent prayer as he was engulfed in flames.

He fell to his knees, then collapsed to the floor without a scream or struggle.

The mirror visage groaned and screamed, finally retreating into its own dimension as the glass melted and finally exploded while the cabin burned.

New England. The Present.

The moon illuminates as the storm wanes and the clouds recede over Fraternity House Row. Inside one of the neat college frat houses, four young college students are partying, drinking, and having a good time.

In a drunken stupor, they draw a pentagram on the floor and sit around it, holding hands. They begin to chant, laughing and giggling at the joke. The sudden sound of a mirror shattering jolts and shocks them.

The last things they hear are sounds of glass slashing and bones breaking, cutting skin, growls, and screams throughout as they are brutally killed by an unseen entity.

A male student has his throat slit, and his hand grasps at the gaping wound as he falls to his knees. He crawls for a few feet, finally collapsing, rolling over onto his back. Blood spills onto the fabric of his letterman's jacket. Another male student is thrown against the wall, and he lands hard on the floor. Blood pours from the back of his head. One eye stares blankly in surprise and death.

A pretty female student tries to run but falls as her legs are sliced and slashed. Her body rests in a pool of her own blood, her face covered by her long, blond hair.

Another female student is frozen in fear, curled up in a corner, unable to move or even scream. The demon turns on her, moving quickly. She lands face down on the floor, head turned to the side. Blood spills onto the back of her light-colored sweater.

They were completely unaware of the supernatural terror that they had just unleashed.

****

The next day on the college campus is a sunny and carefree one. Students scurry around, backpacks over their shoulders and books in hand. Some are jogging and rollerblading around the main dormitory, a large brick building looming on the north side of the campus.

There is an American flag on the roof, a smaller NEU flag nearby, and numerous banners and "sheet-signs" hanging off the sides and front announcing sporting events – including the football season opener, an out-of-town game happening "This Weekend," and other important campus events. Students file in and out through the tall, glass doors.

They mill around the spacious lobby, a comfortable living area for the students to hang out. Some are sitting at tables, while others are stretched out on the floor. All have books and are studying, eating, and talking with their friends. Candy, snacks, coffee, juice, and soda machines abound. A television sits in the corner of the room and is on; a student changes channels with a remote.

Angie Wells, eighteen, shapely and pretty, emerges from the crowd looking angry and a little disoriented. She stops, looks up at the entrance to the dorm building, then sprints up the stairs and hurries in through the glass doors. She has an iPod and headphones and is listening to Ludo.

Angie approaches a table, pulls off her headphones, and flings her backpack down, startling Sarah Norris, Tony Evans, and Robert Goodman. All are clad in the school colors, jackets, and t-shirts.

"Rough day?" Sarah asks her friend.

"Professor Beckman is such an asshole! She locked me out of class today just because I was a little bit late!" Angie sighs.

"How late were you?"

"Just fifteen minutes, but I had a good excuse!"

"Yeah? What was that?" Robert teases.

"I got lost," Angie says sheepishly, shrugging.

"Again?" Tony raises his eyebrows.

"Cut me some slack, I'm a freshman. And she had no reason to lock me out of class. She's just a bitter old bitch," Angie protests as her friends giggle.

"Why don't you just change classes?" Robert asks.

"No other classes were available." Angie shrugs.

"She'd probably get lost on the way to the administration building anyway," Tony chides as the guys collapse with laughter.

"No, I wouldn't! Come on, I'm not that bad," Angie says.

"Yeah, lighten up, guys," Sarah says.

"Okay, so where is the Administration Building?" Robert asks.

"Uhm… Angie looks around, trying to get her bearings. She looks over to Sarah for help, but Sarah only looks around and shrugs. "Uhm, it's…"

"I rest my case," Tony says, laughing. The noisy room gradually quiets down as the students start to watch and listen to the newscast on the television. A pretty newscaster speaks into the camera.

"Police discovered a grisly sight early this morning. The bodies of four New England University students were found in a fraternity house room. The circumstances of these deaths are said to have been very unusual, but officials are releasing few details at this time, and the names of the victims are being withheld, pending notification of relatives. We are going to show you some video now. Please be advised, this is quite graphic footage of a crime scene, which has been described as, quote, a real blood bath." The newscaster speaks professionally into the camera as the kids are transfixed by the broadcast. Other students stop what they are doing and watch.

The newscaster's speech is drowned out as the students focus on the videos of the crime scene, shock and horror overwhelming them as they try to wrap their minds around it all. The covered bodies are wheeled out on gurneys as police put up tape and shoo away the crowd, including the cameraman.

"The victims were apparently stabbed and sliced up by shards of broken glass from a mirror at the scene," her voice continues.

"Creepy," Angie says as she grabs hold of Robert's hand.

"Totally." Sarah watches the newscast with shock and dread.

****

An earlier, shaky shot of the inside shows the pentagram on the floor, mutilated bodies covered in blood, an empty mirror frame, shattered and bloody shards of glass on the floor, and the words "Bloody Mary" partially scrawled on the wall in blood.

Detective Marshall Lewis, mid-fifties and burly looking, is working the crime scene with his partner, Detective Emily Watson, who appears to be in her mid-thirties and attractive. They look up, see the camera, and signal to someone off-screen. A uniformed cop blocks the lens with his hand.

The newscaster continues, "There also were signs of some kind of Satanic cult and a possible ritual being performed. Police have issued no comment on any suspects in this disturbing case. We take you now to…"

The newscast has caught the attention of student Nancy Patrick, a "Goth" type, dark clothes and hair but still attractive in a Morticia Adams kind of way - and not too standoffish, yet still sitting with plenty of empty space around her. She wears a five-pointed star on a chain around her neck, and she rubs it absent-mindedly with her fingers as she watches with growing interest.

Sarah finally has to force her glance away. "My God, that was horrible!

"I know; I saw it earlier," Angie says.

"Can we change the subject?" Robert asks.

"Let's talk about tonight; I want to blow off some steam." Tony grins, stretching his burly body.

"You always want to blow off steam." Sarah gets up from the table, grabbing her backpack.

"Hey, where are you going?" Tony asks.

"Back to the library. I've got a Psych' exam on Monday." The others grab their things and hurry after her.

"Don't tell me you're going to study," Tony says.

"Okay, then I won't tell you." Sarah smiles. They catch up with Sarah, and the four of them amble along. Students wander all around.

Nancy emerges, a worried look on her face. She dials a cell phone and waits a few moments.

"Mom...? You were right; there's something going on here... I'm scared. You have? What do you think it is? I don't know. I've got a lot of classes and... What does dad say? Well, maybe. What should I do in the meantime? I've been doing that. They come and go; it depends. Mom, this is weird. I'm scared, but I'm also drawn to it, you know? It was... You were? Yes, you did tell me; I just never thought that... Okay, I love you guys too. Bye."

She hangs up and puts the phone away. She passes Crazy Ben, bumping into him. They pause, looking at each other for a brief moment, and she can't help but stare at him. The way his scruffy hair frames his face makes him seem scary, yet also slightly familiar. The moment is broken by some skateboarding students whooshing by. When Nancy looks back, Ben is gone.

She ambles along the concrete path between the various buildings. Passing a newsstand, she grabs a copy of the school newspaper.

HEADLINE:
FOUR STUDENTS FOUND DEAD AT DELTA HOUSE.

She curls up her lip in disgust and shoves the paper back onto the rack. As she turns around, she nearly collides with Crazy Ben, who jeers at her.

"You know what they were doing, don't you? You know what they were up to?" Crazy Ben sneers at her

"What? Who?"

"Those kids who were killed. They were doing something they were not supposed to be doing. They were messing around with forces they had no business messing with."

"Leave me alone."

"Don't do it. You will be tempted to do what they did. You will be tempted tonight. Don't do it. Say no."

She tries to shove past him. "I already practice safe sex, and I don't do drugs. At least not the kind you're on!"

"You are doomed if you do. You are doomed. Don't listen. Speak her name, receive her wrath. She doesn't like to be disturbed."

"Yeah, and neither do I. Fuck off!" She shoves past him and hurries on. Crazy Ben watches her as she sprints up the path. He calls after her. "You are doomed!"

**

"We now go live to Police Headquarters, where Chief Thomas is holding a press conference." A serious-looking male newscaster glares into the camera.

Chief Brock Thomas takes the lectern and addresses the crowd with confidence and an air of authority belying a somewhat lack of substance to his words.

"Good afternoon. At this time, we have no suspects, no witnesses, and very few clues to go on. We are asking for any information from anyone who may have seen something last night. Whoever committed these heinous acts was extremely adept at covering their tracks. No physical or DNA traces were found, and there was no sign of forced entry. We believe a Satanic ritual may have played a role in these killings, and we are also looking into a murder-suicide pact as a possible cause of these tragic deaths. We will keep you informed as we learn more. Thank you."

He turns and briskly exits amid a flurry of questions from the reporters.

"…and one of the victims was Mike Sanderson, star linebacker for the NEU football team. Sanderson was scheduled to start in this weekend's season opener against rival Southern New England State, which will be played in the young man's honor. In a related story, some of the parents of the slain NEU students have complained to Chief Thomas about his rush to judgment - suggesting the students had a hand in their own deaths - and the lack of any solid leads in this case. Chief Thomas was unavailable for comment, but a police spokesperson…."

Back in the dorm room, Angie, Sarah, Tony, and Robert are watching.

"Okay, think about it; shattered mirror, pentagram, mutilated bodies… clueless cops… HELLO! It's supernatural or something.," Angie says.

"That's bullshit. A bunch of psycho Goths got out of hand, or maybe they did themselves in, you know, like the cop said… a murder-suicide thing. There's nothing supernatural about this," Robert tells her.

"So, how do you explain the mutilations?" Angie asks.

"They were probably high on Meth or PCP or whatever," Robert says.

"Maybe, but I heard that the bodies were not only slashed but torn apart, like from the inside out."

Tony pipes up. "Oh, you heard, huh? Well, that settles that, doesn't it?"

"Maybe it was Bloody Mary," Angie says.

"Who?" Robert asks.

"You know, the mirror witch."

"The what?!" Sarah asks.

"You go into a dark room, look into the mirror, and say her name three times. Then, she comes out of the mirror to kill you. Haven't you heard about that?" The group just stares at her. "I'm serious! There really is a Bloody Mary."

"Oh, please, that's bullshit," Tony says, shaking his head.

"What if it's not?" Angie asks nonchalantly, shrugging.

"Trust me, Angie; it's bullshit," Sarah says.

"It's just a legend… an urban myth," Tony tells her.

"Okay, if you're so sure, let's try it!" Angie jumps up off her bed,

"Let's not and say we did," Sarah says.

"What are you, scared?" Angie teases.

"Look, I don't want to be stuck in here all night, talking about mirror witches. I want to go grab some brewskis!" Tony gets ups and heads for the door.

"Me too," says Robert. "Come on, Angie."

"You don't believe it anyway, so what's the harm?" Angie asks her friends. The group hesitates, looking at each other. "Then I'll buy the beer, I promise."

"Cool."

"Alright."

"I'm in." Sarah grins as the three of them start closing the shades and turning off the lights. "Let's just get this over with."

"This is gonna be fun!" Angie squeals.

"This is gonna be a complete waste of time." Sarah shakes her head and joins the others. They get the room dark and stand in a semi-circle in front of the mirror over Robert's dresser. They all look to Angie, who remains silent. "So, are you going to call this bitch, or not?"

"Don't call her that!" Angie warns, pointing her index finger at her friend. "You don't want to make her mad."

"Oh, right, I forgot. Don't make the murderous mirror witch mad." Sarah rolls her eyes and stifles a giggle

"Isn't that what we're doing anyway?" Tony asks.

"Shhhhh!" Angie puts her index finger over her lips.

"Sorry," Tony says.

"Okay, here goes." Angie takes a deep breath, and the group holds hands. "Bloody Mary."

The group stares into the mirror.

"Bloody Mary…" Angie continues. They look at their own reflections and see something start to form in the mirror.

"What the…?" Tony squints, trying to make sense of what he sees.

"Shhh! Bloody Mary…" Angie repeats the incantation. The mirror bends and morphs. Slowly, the ghostly visage appears, a sinister grin spreading across its crooked mouth.

"Jesus Christ!" Sarah sucks in her breath, unsure of what she is seeing.

"I don't think so," Tony whispers.

"Not even close," Angie says, her eyes widening at the sight.

"Let's get out of here!" Robert cries. They try to run, but the demon shoots out of the mirror at them. Shards of broken glass join with the smoky demon into a razor-sharp hand, cutting the group into pieces. They scream in terror and try to flee, but it is no use. The demon grabs them and scratches their faces and arms, tearing their bodies to shreds. The small room is a mess of bodies, blood, glass, and the smoky, evil presence. The group falls to the floor in chaos and carnage.

****

It is a sunny morning; the students are going about their business, albeit somewhat more somberly. Someone lays a floral wreath among some others on the steps of the dorm. The entrance is wrapped in crime scene tape.

Dean Carrington is standing at a lectern, addressing a large group of students and press. He is accompanied by Chief Thomas and Detectives Watson and Lewis.

"Everybody calm down. There's no need to feel unsafe here. The police have the situation completely under control." As he speaks, the students boo and protest loudly. "Please, calm down. I've asked Chief Thomas to come here today with his detectives so he can explain how the police are dealing with this situation. Chief Thomas…"

He lets Chief Thomas replace him at the lectern.

"Thank you, Dean Carrington. Now, listen, everyone. We've doubled security around campus, and we're bringing all our resources to bear on this case; that, I can promise you. Detectives Watson & Lewis here are heading up the investigation, and they assure me they're running down every lead and closing in on the killer…" Chief Thomas indicates Lewis and Watson, who smile and wave at the crowd nervously. Watson leans over, speaking quietly to her partner as the Chief continues.

"What leads?" Watson asks her partner. "We don't even have a suspect."

"He's gotta give them something; it's P.R," Lewis replies.

"It's B.S."

"Same thing, different initials."

They both snicker to themselves as Chief Thomas continues. "So, the best thing you can do is go on with your classes and let us handle this situation." He turns the mike back over to the dean as he exits hastily. The crowd assails him with questions; he and the detectives try to calm them down.

They turn their attention back to the lectern, where the crowd has thinned out considerably, and the dean and press have left. Watson spies Nancy and smiles at her.

"Hello, I'm Detective Watson. This is my partner, Detective Lewis."

"Hi, um…" Nancy mumbles back, unsure of herself. She shuffles her feet, looking away.

"Yes?" Watson eyes the girl suspiciously.

"You guys are wrong, okay? You guys are way off here." Nancy blurts out.

"Do you know something we don't?" Lewis asks.

"Yes, I'm pretty sure I do," Nancy answers.

"Do you know who could have done this?" Watson asks.

"It's not a who; it's a what."

"I'm sorry, but I don't follow you," Lewis says. At that moment, Crazy Ben appears out of nowhere. He points to the students and sneers at them.

"People who mess with things they're not supposed to mess with suffer the consequences. You are all doomed. She's disturbed. She was slumbering, and now she has awoken."

"What do you mean, sir?" Lewis asks.

"There are forces in this universe that are not for humans to understand. Those forces are not for drunken college kids to be fooling around with."

"Forces? What forces?" Lewis asks.

"May I get your name, sir?" Watson asks.

"You are doomed! She has been evoked, and she is angry. You are all doomed." Crazy Ben sneers at them.

"Who has been evoked? What are you talking about?" Lewis asks.

"She lives in the mirror, she comes in the dark, she lives for blood." Crazy been glares at Nancy.

"Oh, my God. It IS her!" Nancy shrieks, causing people to stare. She abruptly turns and runs in the direction of the dorm buildings. Josh and Allison walk away as Watson and Lewis eye Nancy and Crazy Ben, who both disappear into the crowd.

Lewis shakes his head and says, "I'll take the old lunatic; you take Morticia, okay, partner?"

"You got it." Watson nods and walks in the direction of the dorms in search of Nancy.

Nancy walks past an open dorm room with students bonging and drinking beer. She swipes away a thick cloud of smoke as a student closes the door. She continues toward her room.

Nancy enters her dorm room and immediately grabs a dusty book from a cluttered shelf. It's a Wiccan book of protective spells. She turns the pages furiously, finally stopping as she arrives at the page she has been searching for…

BLOODY MARY
THE WITCH OF THE MIRROR

Nancy begins to read the pages. After a few moments of silent reading, she is startled by a knock at the door.

"Who is it?" Nancy calls.

"It's Detective Watson; we met outside," a muffled voice answers.

"Okay, just a minute." Nancy quickly shoves the book under her pillow and runs to answer the door.

"Nancy Patrick?"

"Yeah?"

"May I speak with you for a minute?"

"What do you want?"

"Don't be afraid. I'm on your side; I just want to talk to you." Detective Watson's voice is gentle as she speaks to the frightened teenager. Nancy hesitates, then steps aside to let her in.

"My name is Detective Emily Watson." She extends her hand, smiling.

Nancy looks away and clears a space on a chair, nervous and embarrassed. "Hi. I'm sorry, please sit down."

"It's okay," Watson reassures her as she glances around the dorm room.

"Am I in trouble?"

"No, of course not. I want to talk to you about what you said outside."

"You do?"

"Yes. What did you mean when you said we were "way off?"

"Oh, that was nothing. My mom's a... she's into supernatural stuff... I was just clowning around." Nancy shrugs nervously as Watson cocks her head.

"It didn't look like clowning to me. You looked upset."

"I was playing a prank, that's all. I'm uh... I'm pledging a sorority, okay?" Nancy answers the detective nervously, fidgeting with her pentagram necklace.

"Really, which one?"

"I don't remember... There's so many, you know? Keeping my options open..." Nancy trails off as she sits on the bed, exasperated. The book peeks out from under the pillow, but Detective Watson doesn't let on that she's seen it.

"I'll need the name of the sorority for my arrest report," Watson explains.

"What?"

"Obstruction of justice. Your prank interfered with our investigation, so now you are in trouble."

Nancy looks down and tries to cover up the book but realizes it's too late. She reluctantly pulls back the pillow and shows Watson her Wiccan Book.

"Fine. There's no sorority prank," Nancy answers.

"I know. Pledge week was months ago. Besides, you don't strike me as much of a joiner."

"Yeah… So, am I still in trouble?"

"Not if you tell me the truth."

"Here." Nancy hands Watson the book.

"A book of spells?" Watson flips through the pages.

"Do you know anything about this book?"

"I've seen them before. This is New England."

"I'm a Wiccan. That's a book of protective spells my mom sent me."

"Uh-huh…"

"I know it sounds ridiculous."

"Sure does. How would these spells protect you?"

"You're not going to believe me, but I think I know what's going on with these murders."

"Try me."

"What Crazy Ben said today about the entity being disturbed, my mom's psychic dreams, the broken mirrors, now it all makes sense…"

"Yes, it does."

"You mean you believe me?"

"Yes. And if my hunch is right, so-called Crazy Ben may not be so crazy after all."

"But he's just the campus weirdo. Nobody pays any attention to him."

"You seemed to be interested in what he had to say."

"That's because it was true," Nancy tells her.

"You really think so?"

"My mom's never been wrong about this stuff before."

"Mine either."

"You're not like any cop I've ever seen before." Nancy looks over at Watson.

"I'll let you in on an old family secret. I'm actually very familiar with that little book of yours. I was raised in The Faith."

"A Wiccan cop? Cool!" Nancy grins.

"Do me a favor and keep that to yourself, okay? It's not something you want to advertise in my profession," Watson tells her.

"Thanks for telling me. I don't feel so isolated anymore."

"I've denied The Faith and its powers, good and bad, for years. I've been keeping it from my partner, my husband… even myself. "

"I know what you mean."

"But what I saw at those crime scenes could only be the work of a powerful and evil spirit." Watson trails off, looking pensive for a moment.

"And there's only one demon who lives in the mirror."

"Bloody Mary."

"That's right. I need to know exactly what we're dealing with here." Nancy eyes Watson as the detective takes a deep breath.

"Okay, when we found the bodies, there was blood and broken glass everywhere," Watson explains. "They looked like mannequins that had been dipped in red paint. They were the most horrific and gruesome crime scenes that I had ever worked. The second one was worse than the first." She pauses, exhaling loudly.

"I was afraid of that. Go on."

"Shards of glass were sticking up out of their bodies like they had been stabbed from the inside out. That was what started to convince me we were dealing with her…"

"Oh, Jesus."

"Also, on the wall, where the mirror had been, there was a message carved into the blackness."

"'Ye who disturb my slumber shall drip blood for all eternity?" Nancy asks as Watson nods, surprised at Nancy's accuracy.

"That's right..." Watson answers quietly, as if somewhere in the dorm, someone or something may be listening.

"I want to help you. We can defeat her and send her back where she belongs."

"Okay, I'll keep you informed, but for now, let's keep this information between us, okay?"

"Yeah. Thanks, Detective Watson."

"See you later. Stay safe."

"You too." Nancy smiles as Watson leaves, closing the door behind her. Nancy flops down on the bed and sighs loudly.

****

Outside in the quad, Detective Lewis is milling around, talking to students. Detective Watson approaches him as the students walk away.

"Find out anything?" Lewis asks his partner earnestly.

"No, not really, nothing new. You?" Watson eyes the campus quadrangle, keeping watch on any suspicious activity from the students walking by.

"He rambled on about disturbed slumber and impending doom. He's worth keeping an eye on, though. The other students told me he used to be a professor here but got fired under mysterious circumstances."

"That's interesting. What else?"

"Not much. He lives in a basement hovel stocked up for World War Three. He gives me the creeps, but I doubt he could've overpowered those kids. One of them was a varsity linebacker."

"That's true, but let's check him out a little more anyway."

"We'll go back to the station and get on the 'puter."

They make their way to a waiting police cruiser. Watson shakes her head, and Lewis laughs, then pulls out his cell phone and dials as they get in the car. All the while, Crazy Ben has been watching them, peeking from behind a bush.

At the precinct, Detective Watson hurries to her locker and opens it. After rummaging through her things, she finds her old, tattered copy of the same Wiccan book of protective spells that Nancy showed her. She thumbs through it, finding the page about Bloody Mary, marked with handwritten notes in the margin.

"I thought that was you, bitch!" She bookmarks the page and puts the book in her purse.

****

Nancy is in her dorm room, taking it all in. She occasionally has brief and slightly more vivid visions of the 1600s events she describes. She fights the distraction and continues the story.

"During colonial times, some pagans were summoning the mirror witch. They had the last remaining copy of an ancient book of spells. A priest stopped them, destroyed the book, and sent Bloody Mary back to the spirit world where she stayed. Until now."

She suddenly sits up, still in a trance-like state. She stares, transfixed, into a large mirror over the small sink in her dorm room.

From inside the mirror, the glass starts to pulsate, bulge, and change shape.

Suddenly, the eerie visage appears. A pair of angry black eyes appears in the mirror, staring back at Nancy and her friends. A sinister, throaty laugh is heard.

The creature in the mirror grows bigger, and the laugh gets louder. The mirror morphs and cracks, causing Allison and Josh to jump. A glassy hand reaches out to them.

As they turn and try to run, the mirror shatters, and the glassy hand extends and grabs at them. Allison lets out a blood-curdling scream, and Nancy blocks the attack. The grisly hand knocks her aside and aims once again for her friends, who barely make it out of the room.

Nancy looks at the book for a moment, then back at the ghostly apparition appearing before her. With a more serious expression, she realizes the gravity of the situation and knows immediately what she must do. *It's time to get to work.*

"She's getting stronger and more familiar with our world," she whispers to herself, grabbing the book of spells. "Every time she's evoked, it gets easier for her, and she can stay in our dimension longer. Soon, she'll be able to materialize at will anywhere she wants and stay almost indefinitely." With that, she darts frantically out of the room.

Crazy Ben sits cross-legged in front of a huge chalk-drawn pentagram on the floor in his hovel of a home. He reads from an old piece of parchment. It's the torn-out page from the old book of spells.

Crazy Ben looks up to the sky and nods assertively.

"Yes, I know what I have to do." He closes his eyes and begins to chant. "And after all the phantoms are banished, thou shalt see the Holy and Formless Fire... that Fire which darts and flashes to the ends of the universe..."

A distant thunder is faintly heard, along with a slight flash of lightning as a storm gathers strength.

****

Watson is gulping coffee, searching the Internet in her apartment. She begins to have a vision that is similar to Nancy's.

The phone finally rings, and Watson answers.

"It's begun," Nancy says on the other end.

"Okay, thanks. I'm on the way."

Watson dashes out of her apartment. Loud thunderclaps and brief, powerful lightning flashes build in intensity, especially around the dormitory.

****

A television news van arrives, and cameramen & reporters start to set up their equipment. A huge crowd of angry students surrounds the building, while a few uniformed officers and Dean Carrington struggle to keep them back.

Nancy and Detective Watson pull up as the skies are darkened even more and the rain intensifies. They exit the police cruiser and sprint to the front of the building, pushing through the crowd toward one of the officers.

"Please stay calm. We are in the process of providing all of you with temporary housing. When the building is cleared, you can gather your belongings. You will all be sleeping in warm beds tonight, I promise you." Dean Carrington continues addressing the noisy crowd of students as Watson and Nancy walk up to one of the police officers.

"What's going on?" Watson asks.

"The whole building has been vandalized. We had to evacuate the students."

"Okay, keep everyone out."

"Yes, ma'am."

"She's here." Nancy feels the evil presence and sucks in her breath.

"I know. You ready?" Watson asks her.

"Let's do it!" Nancy clutches the book of spells and rubs her five-pointed star. They enter the dorm building and walk through the lobby and hallway.

"Holy Shit!" Nancy starts to gag from a horrible stench.

"Here." Watson hands Nancy a kerchief to put over her mouth. They look around. The whole inside of the lobby is black. They go through the lobby and approach a long hallway, its black walls and ceiling dripping.

The detective pulls out her flashlight and illuminates the dark hallway. On the wall are various pentagrams and symbols. As they continue to walk cautiously through the dark hallway, the writing on the wall gets crazier and stranger.

Meanwhile, Crazy Ben sits in front of the pentagram on the floor, head back, eyes closed, lips moving in silent prayer. Suddenly, his eyes pop open.

"It is time." He puts the page in his jacket pocket and hurries away.

****

The crowd of students is growing agitated and angry. The police and dean try to control the crowd. Crazy Ben appears from the crowd and tries to push past them.

"Nobody's allowed in the building. The Detective is in there," a police officer tells the students as Crazy Ben pulls out the parchment and holds it up.

"The detective can't do anything without…"

"I'm sorry, sir, but you have to stay outside." The officer blocks Crazy Ben from entering.

"You must let me in. I am The Summoner!" Crazy Ben shouts as people start to stare. Dean Carrington looks over at Ben suspiciously.

A few students rush the entrance. A scuffle starts, distracting the officers while Crazy Ben shoves his way into the building unnoticed.

Dean Carrington grows concerned. He looks around and notices Ben has gone, but his attention is soon diverted back to the growing conflict outside the dorm.

Crazy Ben makes his way through the hall, clutching the parchment in his hand and looking around.

"Hello? Hello… anybody there?" Crazy Ben calls out into the darkness. Watson and Nancy look up and around.

"Did you hear that?" Watson asks.

"It sounded like Crazy Ben," Nancy answers, dread in her voice.

"Are you thinking what I'm thinking?"

"I think so, yeah."

"He's the one who…"

"Oh, my God…"

"Hello…?" Crazy Ben calls out again, his voice barely audible, but the women hear him.

"We're in here!" Watson calls out to him.

Crazy Ben looks around at the writing on the walls, squinting his eyes in the dark. He spies a scary-looking message on the wall written in hieroglyphics. He stares at it, and his eyes go wide with terror.

"To seek revenge…" Crazy Ben hurries in the direction of the voices. "Where are you?"

"We're here. Follow our voices!" Watson shouts.

"Ben, is that you?" Nancy yells out to him.

"Yeah," Crazy Ben answers, searching for them in the blackness.

"Can you see my light?" Watson shines her light beam across the wall. It finally finds the face of Crazy Ben, who holds his hands in front of him. "What are you doing here?"

"I am here to help you." Crazy Ben looks concerned and helpless.

"It's much too dangerous for you to be here," Watson tells him, seriously.

"Likewise! This is why I am here." Crazy Ben holds up the parchment and hands it to Nancy.

"This is what was missing. It's from the ancient book of spells!" Nancy inspects the missing page.

"Where did you get this?" Watson shines the flashlight beam on the parchment.

"I want to help you. I summoned her. I just wanted to get even with the school; I never meant for any kids to get hurt. I was just trying to prove… I'm so sorry." He starts to break down, and Nancy comforts him.

"Do you know how to get her back to the other side?" Nancy asks him gently, a friendly hand on his trembling shoulder.

"Yes, it's all there. As the one who summoned her, only I can lure her out," Ben answers with a shaky voice.

"Lure her? With what?" Watson asks.

"A human sacrifice," Ben answers.

"A what!?" Watson looks at him warily.

"He's right. She won't go back unless she gets revenge on the one who disturbed her. Then, when she's vulnerable, we cast the spell that will rid this world of her evil," Nancy explains.

"Correct. Here." He hands Nancy the parchment.

"What do we do?" Watson turns her attention back to Ben.

"When the time comes, read the first part of the spell with me."

Nancy and Watson study the page. Just then, a deafening growl is heard – one so loud that it startles them and sends them to the floor, shaking.

"What the hell was that?" Watson jerks around, shining her flashlight down the empty, dark hallway.

"She's growing angrier. She knows I'm here, but she also knows why I'm here." Crazy Ben begins to dissolve, his body shaking uncontrollably.

"She knows what we're planning?!" Watson asks.

"Maybe… but her thirst for revenge is too strong," Nancy tells her.

"Let's hope so," Watson says, unsure of what exactly is going on but remaining strong.

Suddenly, the hallway explodes into flames, sending the three of them scurrying down the dark hallway. In the illumination from the flames, they see the hallway has changed from black to blood red.

They flee the fire and run deeper into the hallway. A loud shriek is heard, almost like evil laughter. The hallway shakes, and they duck down as burning pieces of the ceiling fall all around them.

"Come on, let's go." Watson runs down the dark hallway as Nancy and Ben follow.

The laughing and shrieking grow louder, and the ceiling starts to drip black and red muck. A slimy remnant drips down inches from Watson's face.

"Jesus!" Watson exclaims, not sure what her eyes are seeing.

"Don't be afraid; she can smell fear," Ben warns as he cringes at the sight.

"Yeah? Well, I bet she's getting a real nostril full right now!"

"Look at this!" Nancy points to an empty space in the wall. They gather around and inspect the odd cavity. It is slowly growing, pulsating, and increasing in intensity.

"The portal. It's getting bigger. Soon, she won't need mirrors or chants anymore," Ben warns as the loud shriek is heard again.

****

As the wicked scream pierces the night, a HazMat truck arrives on the scene, followed by a commander's SUV with its sirens blaring.

Four police officers dart out of the commander's SUV and help the officers control the crowd of students, while the HazMat team prepares to enter the building. Dean Carrington is no longer at the scene.

As the Commander approaches the entrance, the sound of another shriek startles everyone, causing them to freeze in place.

"What the hell was that?" The police commander stares with apprehension in the direction of the building.

"Your guess is as good as mine, sir," the officer answers. "Detective Watson went inside a few minutes ago."

"Alright. You come with me. The rest of you stay here and keep these kids outside. Give orders to hold off until you hear from me and keep those Goddamn reporters back. Let's go." The Commander and the police officer enter the building with guns and flashlights drawn as the others hold back the increasingly agitated crowd.

The police enter cautiously. Their eyes go wide with terror as they see the black mess inside.

"What the hell happened in here?" The police officer gazes around with shock and horror.

"Come on," the commander orders as they proceed through the building. "Detective Watson...?"

Nancy, Detective Watson, and Crazy Ben hear the commander's voice.

"Stay back!" Watson shouts.

The police officers hold their flashlights out, following the beam.

"Detective Watson, are you okay?"

"I'm fine. Stay back," Watson answers. Suddenly, the loud growling is heard again. The police officers stop in their tracks and look around, turning their flashlights and guns toward the sound.

The officer stammers through shallow breaths. "W-what was that?" Out of the darkness, the demon appears. The growling gets louder and louder until it seems to surround the officers, who shriek in terror.

"Let's get the hell out of here!" The commander watches as the monster has them trapped in a corner. They are powerless to stop it. They fire their guns at it, but it's no use. The officers scream in horror as the monster pounces on them, tossing them around like rag dolls, slashing them to pieces.

Nancy, Watson, and Crazy Ben start looking around when they hear the cries of the police officers. Then, a loud, crunching sound is heard.

"She got them." Crazy Ben shakes his head as he removes a piece of white chalk from his pocket, draws a pentagram on the ground, and steps into the center of it. "We'd better get started. Are you ready?"

"Ben, are you sure you know what you're doing?" Watson asks him.

"Yes. I must sacrifice myself to lure her away from our world."

"Ben, no! There has to be another way, please!"

"There's no other way. It's my fault, I have to make things right."

"What can we do?" Watson asks helplessly.

"There's nothing else we can do. He's settling his karmic debt," Nancy clarifies as Watson looks on.

"We must begin now. It has started." Ben looks at Nancy and Watson, and they nod silently. Nancy pulls out the parchment. As Ben begins the spell, the girls join in.

"Oh, demon from the darkest depths of Hell, you must depart the earthly plane. You have no place among the mortal, go back and return nevermore. Nans lum bek hans ba sha…" They all chant together as the loud growling is heard again. Nancy and Detective Watson hold hands.

"Remove your evil poison from this dimension. We compel you with the power of this Earth, the wisdom and love of the Supreme Being, and all that is good in the heart & soul of man. We condemn you back to the bowels of Hell and into the arms of Satan from whence you came. Nans lum bek hans ba sha… Nans lum bek hans ba sha…"

"Oh, my God!" Watson exclaims in shock and horror as a small fire begins to form a circle around the pentagram. Crazy Ben stands with his hands together, as if in prayer. The growling gets louder and louder.

"Pray for my soul." Crazy Ben looks over at Nancy and Watson, retreating from the heat and flames. He continues the incantation as a smoky hint of the demon begins to be drawn in. "Evil Bloody Mary, witch of the mirror, mistress of death, I command you to leave this world immediately. Take me now, the one who awoke you, and satisfy your hunger. Nans lum bek hans ba sha…"

As he and the girls repeat the chant, the fire grows in intensity. Nancy and Watson are forced back as the demon begins to materialize, darting in and out of the growing inferno, attaching to and retreating from Ben, winding around him, and fighting to get away… thrashing, struggling, and weakening.

"Take my flesh, blood, and body for your revenge and return to peaceful slumber forever. Nans lum bek hans ba sha… Nans lum bek hans ba sha…" Ben continues the incantation. The fire begins to get bigger, and the growling gets louder as the group looks on. They watch in fascination as the fire begins to engulf Crazy Ben, and he cries out in pain and terror.

The demon wraps itself around Ben, trying to pull him away but being engulfed in the growing inferno along with him. It howls and thrashes angrily, threatening the others but unable to break free.

The parchment is sucked from Nancy's grasp and disappears into the growing, swirling inferno. The flames shoot out from all around Crazy Ben as the growling grows deafening. Nancy and Watson cover their ears, repeating the chant louder as Crazy Ben and the demon are engulfed in the flames. His cries of terror and the demon's screams fill the air. Suddenly, the flames disappear, and the hallway is quiet. A few last wisps of smoke linger briefly, then are gone.

"Where did he go?" Watson asks as they stare down at the black spot on the ground where Crazy Ben once stood. There is no sign of him.

"He's gone." Nancy reaches down and touches the spot where he once was. It's as if nothing was ever there. A single shard of glass shines in the moonlight, revealed by the retreating clouds as the storm and rain subside.

Watson shines her light around the area. "They're both gone." She gazes around the room.

"Look!" Nancy points over at the ooze and stickiness, which are receding... color returning to the walls and floors. The shard of glass is sucked into the shrinking vortex as the portal closes up, and the wall returns to normal. "It worked!"

"I say we get the hell out of here," Watson tells Nancy as they make their way down the empty hallway.

***

The crowd outside the building is a mix of students, police, news reporters, and various looky-loos. The detective and Nancy step out into a madhouse of people. The police try to move the crowd away from the front of the building as Watson and Nancy are led to a nearby ambulance.

Chief Thomas arrives and takes control; all the cameras and media attention turn to him as he turns on his P.R. charm.

"There have been many new developments in this case in the last few hours. If you'll just bear with me, I'm going to bring over our lead detective…" He beckons to Watson, who holds up her index finger. He nods hesitantly and continues, "…uhm Detective Watson, who will be joining me shortly…"

Watson grabs some water bottles and hands one to Nancy. They swig the water heartily as an EMT starts to work on Nancy's minor injuries.

"I'm fine; check on her," Watson tells a paramedic who immediately approaches her.

"Just another day at the office?" Nancy teases as she gulps more water.

"Hardly! I demand a raise after this case." Watson nods as they laugh and share a look.

Watson looks over at the crowd. Chief Thomas struggles with the reporters and looks over at her, beckoning toward her.

"Right. Thanks for everything, Detective Watson." Nancy smiles.

"It's Emily, Nancy. Please call me Emily. We're friends and sisters of The Faith, forever."

"Thanks, Emily." Nancy smiles.

They hug, and Nancy heads off into the night. Watson joins Chief Thomas with the reporters.

Chief Thomas introduces Watson and hands her the microphone. For a brief moment, his sleeve rises, revealing a pagan tattoo on his lower left forearm, though nobody notices.

Nancy turns back to look once more at the dorm. She stares with apprehension as she sees a faint shadow in one of the dark windows. She reaches up and touches her necklace.

"And it harm none, do what ye will." Nancy quickly jerks her gaze away. As she walks toward the police cruiser, she stops and grabs her head, steadying herself against a parked car. Nancy has new visions. Quick flashes of a mirror shattering, young voices screaming, and carnage. Indistinct and abstract but unmistakable.

Nancy is distraught and tries to shake the visions away, running down the path. She runs off as the torn, missing page from the ancient book of spells is floating in the wind.

Hidden Consequences
By Katie Jaarsveld

Gran's last request was for Sasha to locate objects hidden
in the walls and under the floorboards. The first of these
was a weathered old book. She soon learned not to read the
contents aloud, no matter how delicious the results.

Prologue

My mother, Natalie, and I went to live with my Grandma Natasha when I was young. I loved exploring our house as a child. There were all sorts of objects, magic, and when the three of us were together, it was almost as if the house had come to life. Gran said it was because there were three generations of witches in the house at one time… a maiden, a mother, and a crone… Sasha, Natalie, and Natasha. I liked the idea of being a witch. I mean, what child wouldn't?

Shortly after we moved in, my mom fell ill and died. She kept talking about needing her tiger eye necklace, but it was not found until she no longer needed it.

The house became still after mom passed on. Gran and I did a special service with women I remembered from my childhood. Gran said they were her coven.

I wore my mom's tiger eye necklace, which I'd found in her slipper beside her bed. I guess it had fallen in there at some point. I just wished she had been able to wear it one more time. Wearing mom's necklace, it felt like she was still with me, and gran said she could feel her too. The house regained some of its warmth after I started wearing it.

Gran told me that not all magic was good, but I knew that. Mom repeated it often enough. Gran admitted that dark magic was the reason for our grief. Then gran passed away, and the house took on a gloom as if it were in mourning as well. The stone in gran's ring cracked when she passed on.

After that, I found that my interest in magic had diminished. I was never really as serious about it as mom and gran. I knew basic spells and felt a sense of belonging when I cast them, but without my family, it just wasn't the same.

Gran left me all her possessions and our house, which needed some minor repairs. She also sent me on a scavenger hunt to find missing articles. The idea was confusing to me at the time.

The Scavenger Hunt

Being older didn't necessarily mean wiser. I was going from room to room on a scavenger hunt, as requested by my gran shortly before her passing. It didn't make sense to me, but if it helped me and our home, I was all for it.

Gran also wanted me to believe in the power of magic again and develop a true love for it. I always felt better after casting, so I'd give it a try. For mom and gran. Perhaps it would even help me to repair gran's ring that she loved so much. Even with a cracked stone, I wore it. Mom's tiger eye never left my neck.

I had found mom's necklace in her room, so maybe I'd find the next object in gran's room. I still had no idea what I was looking for, as there hadn't been a list. I was on my own. I figured I'd get a feeling for it at some point.

Stepping over the threshold into gran's room, I noticed that there was a creaky floorboard. I lifted the rug and found a loose board. When I lifted it up, I found something wrapped in an old, burlap cloth. I pulled it out and made sure nothing else was hidden there. Satisfied it was empty, I replaced the board and rug. Gran was all about tidiness, and I'd inherited that from her. I couldn't focus in a dirty room.

I carefully unwrapped what felt like a book. The dust made me sneeze three times, which made me smile. Gran's favorite number was three, for us three.

Her spell book. She told me she had misplaced it. Gran had loved teasing me. She knew I wasn't ready to see the book, at least until I was serious about magic.

I opened the book, carefully running my hand over its pages. My hand felt as if it were being tickled by a gentle electricity. The book was leather-bound by hand, and the pages at the beginning were yellowed, containing very old entries. All the pages were handwritten. There was a section labeled with gran's name, then newer entries stating mom's name with her handwriting.

I looked at many blank pages, waiting to see if anything appeared. I was really disappointed when nothing showed. I ran my fingers over mom's last entry, then writing started to appear on the following page. My name was now in the book. Did that mean it was my time to make spells and entries? I didn't know how. I hadn't paid attention. The thought made me sad. I should have listened.

I took off mom's necklace and held it as I started to cry and apologize, rubbing the cracked stone in gran's ring.

"Hush now, child. This is no time for regrets; they do nothing but make it harder for you to heal."

Gran. She had said the same thing when mom died. I could *feel* her talking more than I could *hear* her. I knew gran was still with me. I never understood why mom wasn't.

"If we were both here all the time, you wouldn't move on with life. You'll hear your mom when you're ready to hear her. But you need to return to our ways. Your mom is trapped and cannot communicate with the living or the dead. The thing that killed her holds her tight. Be strong and learn, child. For all our sakes."

Her voice drifted away, and I smelled her patchouli. I wiped my tears with my hands and felt a shock on my left index finger. Gran's ring was glowing with a spiral of light around it. When the light dissipated, I looked at the ring and saw that the Lapis Lazuli was healed.

"Well done, child. Your tears healed the stone, opening the third eye to deep wisdom and enlightenment."

My heart felt lighter, and for the first time in a long time, I felt stronger.

I gently laid the book on gran's bed. Tapping on the walls and floors, I heard and felt nothing that didn't belong. I picked up the book and took it with me to mom's room. There weren't any carpeting or boards out of place, even under the bed with the dust bunnies. Apparently, I needed to sweep.

There was a picture I hadn't seen before on her nightstand. Actually, it was more like a watermark. I decided to open the frame and take a closer look. It was mom but more of a shadow of her. Gran had said mom was trapped.

I took off her tiger eye and wrapped it around the picture without bending it. The book opened with great force, and pages began flipping, faster and faster. I smelled patchouli, then lavender. Gran and mom's scents. Mom was here.

The pages flipped back and forth. I didn't know which of them were searching for what, but they disagreed about its location in the book. If they didn't stop soon, I was going to make tea. The book stopped and closed. Didn't it contain what they needed?

I picked up the book and held it in my hands. Closing my eyes, I opened the book with the front and back cover, not touching the pages as they began to flip back and forth once again. I left my eyes closed until the pages stopped moving. I had been muttering something under my breath, but I had no idea what I was saying.

The book opened to a Raidho Rune R. Mom kept her runes in a wooden bowl on her bookcase so they could breathe and stay energized. I scanned it for keywords. Astral travel obtains justice, brings progress, moves energies, and gives them direction. Great! Now I just need to cast the spell.

I won't lie; I was nervous. Mom's dresser had served as an altar in the past. As a matter of fact, most of her things were still there. I just needed to remove the non-essential items. Most of her room was the same. It didn't matter if we moved something, it always came back to her room. I used to move things around the room for fun when I was younger, but they were back in their place before I exited her room.

With the candles, crystals, her picture, her necklace, herbs, incense, oils, and chalice, I was ready. I found the page that I needed, with a spell intended to call upon the elements and summon the goddess. I chanted words I did not know, somehow feeling the spell deep in my core without ever having learned it. When the wind died down, the candles extinguished, and the room felt light.

I laid the book down on the bed and looked at mom's picture. It was mom, not a shadow. It had worked. I placed her necklace around my neck and placed her photo back in the frame. The book was opened to my name, and there was writing in my hand. The spell I had cast was now in the book.

I felt someone touch me, and I jumped, stifling a scream. Positive it was only mom or gran, I turned around with a smile. I froze. There was a man standing there with no shirt on. His bulging muscles made my heart race.

He looked like he was going to devour me; instead, he walked past me and reached for my book. I uttered a few words, and an invisible barrier formed between him and the book, not allowing him to even step closer, let alone touch it.

He looked at me and, with a guttural cry of frustration, reached for my throat. I barely breathed some words just as he was making contact with my skin. His hand was half-way through the same type of barrier and had become stuck. He hooked his finger on my necklace and let out a yelp of surprise. I felt a tingle, but I think he felt a shock. He jerked his hand back, shattering the wall.

As he stood in front of me, he transformed. He was still very cute but not as muscular; he was shorter but still do-able. I closed my eyes just for a second and wished him away. When I opened my eyes, he was gone. I'd almost missed him, the second him. What was I saying? The first him would have killed me. Besides, I didn't know who or what he was, but he wanted the book.

I reached for the book and felt my hand go through something I can only describe as a whisper. Every spell I was saying was now in the book. At least I didn't have to write them down and risk messing up a page. I had to find someplace safe to hide the articles as I found them.

But how did he enter my house? That was something I needed to deal with first. Gran always placed protective spells around the house with salt and stones. I remembered us three tending to them. I guess I had been remiss in keeping up with things. I'd take care of that, then go back to the scavenger hunt.

I went to the basement and wrapped the book and mom's picture in a blanket, then laid them in the dryer. The mysterious stranger wouldn't think to look in the dryer, would he? I grabbed a big bucket of salt, along with a spade and water. The salt didn't need to be seen in order to work. Gran always buried some around the crystals, and at a halfway point between them. This salt was a mix of varieties and sizes for strength and potency. Everything from table salt to rock salt. I checked on the position of the quartz crystals as I spread the salt and found two out of line.

It took a couple of hours, but the job was done. I also spread salt mixed with brick dust at the windows and doors. As long as the stranger was outside, he wouldn't be able to re-enter so easily.

My task completed, I decided on a quick shower before resuming the scavenger hunt. While I didn't mind smelling of salt, it did tend to itch a bit under the shirt, especially with the brick dust mixed in. I didn't know where the little windstorm came from, but it certainly assisted me in my task. Contrary to popular belief, once salt was placed, you couldn't just wipe it or blow it away, especially since I'd added a little water to soak some into the wood.

I put on comfortable shorts and a tank top, then made a peanut butter and jam sandwich and a glass of sweet tea. It was unusually warm outside. The cicadas would be signaling nightfall soon, with a back chorus of bullfrogs. The leaves were changing colors, and I could almost smell autumn. As I ate my sandwich, the lights scattered around the property came on.

The neighbor's lights weren't as bright as they usually were, but the lights on the pathway to the house were solar-powered and worked fine, as did the lights surrounding points at the house. I'd added salt around them too for good measure.

Desdemona and the Wolf

I needed to gather the things from the scavenger hunt and continue finding the rest. As far as I could tell, the outside of the house was secure, depending on who or what wanted in. I put mom's necklace back on, placed the book and mom's picture under a loose board in the pantry, and set grans cauldron on top for good measure. I thought about lighting the fireplace.

The fireplace. It wasn't cold enough for a fire. I ran to the fireplace. It had been swept clean after it was too warm to light it. I pulled the heavy grate forward, and Aunt Tilly's black cat jumped out at me and hissed. It was a good thing I hadn't drank all my tea or, it would have been running down my leg.

Aunt Tilly wasn't really my aunt; she was part of gran's coven. Desdemona, her cat, hadn't been seen around here since gran died. Desdemona was more gran's cat than Aunt Tilly's. She rolled onto her back, demanding that her belly be rubbed. There was something on her collar. I rubbed her belly and unhooked a crystal from her collar. While I checked it out, Desdemona went back to grooming her paw.

I rubbed it and instantly felt like someone had hit the back of my head with a sledgehammer. No one was there, and I was fine. I was 'seeing things.' I'd had premonitions as a child. After mom died, gran and her coven did something that made it quiet. I remembered everything. They had placed my memories and premonitions in this crystal.

Desdemona must have had it attached to her collar this whole time. I attached it to mom's chain. There would be more strangers coming to the house; they wouldn't be who they said they were. They would be able to enter the yard but unable to enter the house.

I held the crystal, tiger eye, and ring with one hand. With the power of us three, I cast a protection spell over the house and its contents. That included me as well as Desdemona. She curled up on the blanket I'd draped over gran's favorite chair.

There was a wolf howling outside. I remembered him. He was an immortal friend of gran's. He'd scratched me as a child; I had the scar on my leg to prove it. It never really hurt, though. He smelled like a combination of wet dog and skunk. His fur was not like Desdemona's; it had thick strands and a wiry texture. Mom was worried about the repercussions, but gran assured her that I would live a long, healthy life with a pack as my guardians. Gran had saved his pack from man a long time ago.

Anyone who was true to the family would be able to come in. Anyone with ill intent would not be kept out. I took a deep breath and opened the door. He was walking up the steps slowly, giving me time to get used to him, I think. He winked at me.

After he was in, he ran downstairs and came back up dressed and in his human form. I didn't remember him looking that handsome in all my twenty years... or twenty-one, rather. It was at that moment that I fully realized that I was turning twenty-one the following day – and what that meant. I remembered gran saying that I would gain my full powers on my twenty-first birthday.

I shook my head, my thoughts returning to Renae. He smiled at me, and I ran into his arms. That was my first contact with anyone since gran had died. It was good to see him, but the relief at having someone I could trust was overwhelming. I started to cry, and he held me. I felt him stroking my hair and whispering comforting words. He kissed the top of my head.

Then I remembered something else and slowly backed away from him. On my twenty-first birthday, I was to marry into the wolf pack, with my being a half-breed since my father was a wolf too. Mom had lost some of her powers when she married, then regained them when she became pregnant with me. Their union had established peace within the pack and gran's coven.

He sat on the sofa, and Desdemona jumped up on his lap for attention. Had everyone lost their minds? A cat liking a wolf? Really. I needed a moment to think while Renae and Desdemona were communicating. I went to the kitchen to get a drink. Desdemona requested some warm milk. Another memory. This house was a safe haven for telepaths. Anyone residing within these walls didn't need to speak out loud.

Anyone residing in this house. Desdemona did stay here, whenever she chose to do so. Did that mean Renae would be residing here as well? He did have belongings downstairs. I was developing a headache.

I took iced tea for Renae and myself, along with some chicken sandwiches, and warm milk with a plate of chopped chicken for the cat. I set the refreshments down and sank into a chair to contemplate any changes.

I could see they were still catching up, so I tucked my legs under me in the chair and closed my eyes for a moment. More wolves were coming; they weren't a threat. Witches were coming from all directions. It was for my marriage ceremony in the back yard.

I woke up with someone shaking me. Renae. I'd had another premonition. It would take some time for me to get to those again.

"Renae, who am I to marry tomorrow?"

My voice was so low that I wasn't sure if he could hear me. Desdemona sat straight up. I had her attention. His head was hanging.

"I thought you knew. It was always meant for you to marry me. I was your father's successor when he died. I was young and challenged by others over the years, but it is my pack. Just as you are."

He spoke with conviction and possessiveness. Desdemona winked at me, circled her pillow three times, then lay down to nap. I didn't know what to say, so I said nothing. He sat back down with the cat and stroked her fur. Her purring reminded me of my childhood.

She was batting a stick around. It had crystals and strange markings on it. Remembering was like being tortured. The pieces were there, but someone had hidden parts of the puzzle. Desdemona had a crystal. *I wonder-*

I stood so fast that both Renae and Desdemona jumped. I pulled the grate back out, and at the back, covered by soot, was the stick with crystals. I wiped it off with my napkin. There were symbols inscribed into the wood.

Before Renae could stop me, I read it out loud. The same man as before was standing before me. Oh, shit! So, he didn't come into the house; I had summoned him.

"Read the words backwards! Hurry!"

Yeah, easier said than done. Renae held onto him, but the demon was a match. Standing next to Renae, he looked more muscular, but his appeal wasn't there. I didn't know what I was thinking.

"Today, Sasha! I don't know how much longer I can hold him."

Just as he broke loose from Renae's grip, I repeated the words three times. I heard a yell and saw black dust explode in the room. Desdemona let out a screech and took a dive under the sofa. The blast knocked Renae backward. When he stood, he was a wolf again. I stood there, not sure what to do. He sent me a telepathic message.

"Instinct."

He ran downstairs. While he was gone, I fetched the vacuum and proceeded to clean up. I was almost finished when he made an appearance, looking fresh from the shower and without a shirt or shoes. I heard a whistle, and if I didn't know better, I'd say it came from the cat. I looked at her and nodded in agreement.

I went into the other room to the cabinet with gran's vials in it. I decided to scoop up some demon essence, just in case. You never knew what you would need for a potion.

I kept looking over at Renae. He hadn't fastened the button on his jeans yet. I loved the pathway to...

"Sasha!"

I couldn't help but choke on a laugh. Busted by Gran. Desdemona must have heard her since she was meowing and having a fit like a normal cat. Gran's spirit appeared. She had never done that with me before.

"So, child. You approve of your mate?"

I didn't know ghosts could laugh, but here was gran, having a laugh at my expense.

"Why didn't you tell me? Why wipe my memories? What's with you all suspending my premonitions, and who the hell was the demon?"

"I didn't tell you about your marriage because I was supposed to be here to perform the ceremony. I wiped your memories because you weren't dealing with your mom's demise. He was the same one who killed your dad, by the way. I suspended your premonitions because I didn't want you to watch me die. The demon, you, and Renae had to be together for him to die. Well done, you two. You might want to keep demon dust. It's hard to come by but extremely useful. Just don't tell anyone you have it."

I sat down so hard that I almost missed the edge of the sofa.

"Did you find all nine objects yet?"

"Nine? I found mom's necklace, repaired your ring, the book, restored her in her picture, the crystal the cat had, along with the inscribed crystal wand that I used to kill the demon. I'm missing three items."

"Actually, no. You're missing one item."

I thought about it for a moment. I understood what she meant, and what the last item was.

"Desdemona and Renae were two, but they found me, not the other way around. I'll be right back."

I ran upstairs to my room. When I was given news of my father's death, I was presented with the pack crest, his medallion. I would need to give it to Renae for a wedding gift if he accepted my proposal. I was going to propose. I stood there, frozen. If gran hadn't messed with my memories, I would be ready for this day… or maybe not. But it's here, and I feel a bond to Renae. I pocketed the medallion. I was happy with my decision, and I hoped he would be too.

Aunt Tilly

I heard a commotion downstairs and ran to see what it was. Aunt Tilly was there, and Desdemona was scratching her. Renae had a deep scratch on his arm and was fighting the urge to shift. Wolves would not interfere with witch conflicts and vice versa.

Something was wrong. I couldn't see or hear gran. Desdemona leaped on Tilly and tried biting her. Where was the wand? I saw it hidden just under the cushions where Desdemona was sitting. I ran for it, but my motion caught Tilly's attention. She reached for me, and Renae intercepted… as a wolf. She screamed, and I heard others coming. This was not going to be good.

I said the words three times backwards, but Tilly was still there.

"Stupid child! Did you think that would affect me when I'm holding this?"

She held out the book and mom's picture. *How did she find them? How do I get them back?* I sat on the sofa, not letting her know about the wand. I had all nine pieces now, and I intended to keep them.

"I was there when your grandmother pulled the board to keep things safe. I've always known. I counted on all nine things, plus you, being accessible to me. I would be the most powerful witch alive, far surpassing even your grandmother. I made the potions that killed your mother so slowly. She didn't get sick until she moved here, did she? Then there was your grandmother; she should have died a long time ago, but she recovered from every attempt I made on her life. I promise, you won't have to marry that dog, and you can even join the coven. Maybe we'll have a sacrificial cat."

Tilly didn't understand that it was the three of us that made us all so powerful. Not the items but each other being who we were. I tried to communicate that to Desdemona and Renae. I stood up quickly, grabbing the wand; meanwhile, Desdemona jumped on Tilly's face, causing her to drop the picture and the book. I ran over and grabbed them while Renae pinned her face down on the floor, with Desdemona standing on her head.

I started chanting, and someone outside yelled for me to stop. It was the coven, with the wolf pack close behind them. Could this day get any better? I looked down and started to laugh. It wasn't funny, but it was. A woman face down on the floor, with a wolf standing on her back and a cat sitting on her head. I communicated my thoughts to Renae and Desdemona.

Renae was struggling to resist laughing; no longer able to control himself, he began returning to his very male, naked form. Desdemona was snickering, if you could call it that coming from a cat. She pressed her claws into Tilly's face. Half of the wolf pack ran to the back of the house, returning as men with clothes on. The other half stayed as wolves near the witches.

I didn't know what the rest of Renae looked like, but I was finding the view of his backside quite enjoyable. He sent me a silent plea for help; I hesitated, then smiled and nodded. He grabbed a pillow, tossed it at me, and ran downstairs before the men were at the front door.

I asked the coven why they couldn't come closer. One of the wolves howled. There were more witches coming up from behind. The wolf pack surrounded the witches, who could not enter. They started to shimmer. They weren't witches at all but demons, and they were having a hard time keeping their shape. I yelled for Renae, and when he saw what was happening outside, he and the others shifted back into wolves.

A younger wolf was standing on Tilly, but she was shimmering too. I asked Renae to take care of her. I needed to cast a spell and fast! I thought of gran. I had the demon dust. I grabbed it and a few dried ingredients. Mixing them together, I conjured a wind around the ones who shimmered. I hoped I had enough to take care of them all.

I started with Tilly. With my incantation and a little dust, she was a pile of ash. I sent the rest of the demon dust on a breeze to the ones in the circle of wolves. The demons were changing form, and the wolves had their heads lowered, probably because they knew something was coming.

The demons disintegrated into a pile of dust... no explosion or dramatics, just dust. The witches walked up behind them and requested some of the dust for the coven. After they proved they could step into the protection circle, I allowed it.

Epilogue

Two of the wolves stood guard as the rest ran into the house to change once again. Once they returned, some of the witches came to the porch and introduced themselves. The others were making certain no demon came back from the ashes.

I recognized several of the witches from gran's meetings. I heard horses, then saw wagons full of kegs, food of all kinds, and animals for wedding presents. I didn't look at Renae. I asked everyone to excuse us for a moment and led Renae inside.

After closing the door, I reached into my pocket. I took both of his hands in mine, with the medallion pressed into his left hand. I could feel the electricity pass between us. There were no words; none needed to be spoken.

The Priestess opened the door and announced we were married. We kissed and heard howls and laughter. The Priestess closed the door on her way out, and the festivities commenced. As for Renae and I, we weren't thinking about food.

Dead Girls Don't Cry
By J.M. Goodrich

Three best friends decide to get revenge on the girl who's been tormenting them. Secretly, they've been dabbling in witchcraft, drawn to its addictive and seductive power. Will their revenge be everything they hoped, or will there be dire consequences?

Chapter One

"Hey, Rose, do you still have that perfume I like… the one I borrowed last time I was over?" asked Lana. She could hear objects being moved around through the speakerphone. She and her best friend, Rose, spoke to each other on the phone every morning while getting ready for school.

"I think so; let me check… the one in the blue bottle, right? Shaped sort of like a teardrop?"

"That's the one. If you find it, can I borrow it again, please?"

More rustling. "Found it!" Rose yelled triumphantly. "I'll bring it with me. You really should buy your own, though."

Lana laughed. "Thanks, girl. I owe you one." She turned to Jade, who was sitting on her bed, examining her nails. "I really should buy my own stuff. I'm always bumming things off you guys." She shrugged, then hung up the phone and tossed it in her purse.

Jade looked up at her friend. "You know we don't mind," she said, smiling. She returned her focus to her nails as she continued, "I don't know about you, but I just don't feel like going to school today. Let's ditch." She shifted, tucking her feet underneath her.

"You know, I would love to, but my parents would so kill me," Lana responded, brushing out her long hair.

"I'm just so sick of Queen Veronica and her posse. You'd think they could let up on the teasing every now and then. Just once, I'd like to be able to walk around school and not have to worry about rumors or garbage being dumped on my head in the cafeteria or dead animals being shoved in my locker." She shuddered at that last thought.

"I know what you mean," Lana admitted, sighing. "She's never been nice, but this year she kicked the bitchiness up a few notches."

Jade laughed.

"This is our senior year, though," Lana continued. "Maybe she'll cool off soon."

"Doubt it. You know her... not happy until everyone around her is miserable."

Lana couldn't argue that. Instead, she shrugged and grabbed her bag, motioning for Jade to follow.

****

Lana drove both her friends to school, and they sat at their usual bench outside as they awaited the first morning bell. Rose settled in, practically bouncing in her seat as she asked, "When do you guys want to go shopping for Halloween costumes?"

Jade took off her sunglasses to address her friend. "Don't you think we're a little too old to be dressing up?"

"You're never too old for Halloween," Rose shot back.

Lana just laughed as she lay in the sun, enjoying the unseasonably warm weather.

"You freaks are too old for everything," a voice called out. The girls looked up to see Veronica standing before them with a sneer on her face. "And it's not like the three of you need a costume. You're scary and freaky-looking enough as it is." Her followers laughed.

The three friends sat there, silently. They had learned not to engage Veronica in any sort of conversation. She would always win.

Veronica tossed her hair over her shoulder. "What's wrong? Black cat got your tongue?" She laughed again, then kneeled down to stare into Lana's face. "The three of you will never be anything other than the nasty, disgusting freaks that you are. No one will ever accept you. No one will ever love you." She continued staring Lana in the eye, waiting for her to speak, but Lana bit her tongue and held in her boiling rage.

Finally, Veronica straightened up. "I'm done with you freaks." She turned on her heel and walked away.

"Oh, I hate her so much," Jade said once she was out of earshot.

"Me, too," said Lana. "She needs to be taught a lesson. This has gone on long enough." She turned to her friends, her eyes glistening in the sunlight as she beamed with ideas. "What do you say we meet up at the old house this weekend and come up with something special for her?"

"I like that idea," Rose replied with a mischievous grin on her face.

"Count me in," said Jade, giving Veronica one more look. "It's about time someone took that bitch down."

Chapter Two

Saturday couldn't come soon enough. The girls had spent every day after school researching spells, looking for the perfect one to take care of their little bully problem.

They went out to their favorite place to hang out: an old, abandoned house in the middle of the woods. It was run down and kind of smelly, but it suited their needs perfectly. No one ever bothered them there. No one else knew of its existence.

It was so old that the forest had begun to reclaim it; from the outside, it just looked like an enormous mass of trees and moss at first glance. The girls had stumbled upon it by accident one night while wandering around the woods after having a little too much to drink.

After frequent, uninterrupted visits, the girls claimed it as their own. It was their sanctuary, a place where no one could bother them. They were free from bullies and insults – free to just be themselves. Out there, they were free to work on their witchcraft.

After discovering it the previous summer, they were drawn to its seductive power. It's what drew them to each other, and the three of them have been inseparable ever since.

****

Lana picked up the other two girls since she was the only one who had a car, and they headed out once again to their secret spot. They were nearly bursting with excitement, having studied witchcraft for a little over a year, though they had yet to actually cast a spell. This would be their first.

When they arrived, Rose set out a fresh bowl of food and water by the front door for Spirit, the black cat that occasionally hung around the house.

"Why don't you just adopt the thing?" Jade asked her.

Rose let out a sigh. "You know I'd love to, but my dad is deathly allergic to cats."

"Or so he says."

"No, he really is," Rose insisted, nodding. "I've been trying for years to get him to let me have a pet."

"Well, that's too bad then," shrugged Jade.

"Yeah, but old Spirit here is good enough for me. I still get to take care of the little guy and love on him." She smiled and led the way into the house.

Lana located the Book of Shadows containing all their spells, while Jade lit a few candles around the room. They had them stashed all over the house, both for use in spells and for light since there was no electricity running out there.

****

The Book of Shadows was something that Lana had found tucked away in her attic. She didn't know whose it was… just that it had belonged to someone in her family. On the cover was her family crest and her last name. But that was it – no first name or even a mention of anyone else's name anywhere in the book.

Every page was filled with spells, incantations, and ingredients. Every inch was covered in cramped handwriting, making most of it almost impossible to decipher.

Lana had been sitting at home by herself when she felt something calling to her from the attic. The call was so strong, she just couldn't ignore it, so to the attic she went, snooping around until at last, she had located the book. She swore it vibrated at her touch, and she knew it was special – that it was the very thing that had been beckoning to her.

It cemented the feeling she'd already had about being meant for more. She'd always been drawn to witchcraft, feeling as though that was her true calling. As she studied, she found comfort and meaning in the texts.

The three friends practiced in secret and swore never to tell another soul about their newfound passion. No one would understand, and they were teased enough as it was.

Each girl had their own personal, albeit similar, experiences that led them to believe in witchcraft and feel drawn to it as though it had always been a part of them deep down.

****

Rose had been upset one day after being turned down yet again during one of her pleas for a family pet. She was always so gentle and nurturing. She just wanted a little puppy or kitty of her very own to love and to always be there for her. She hated being alone and longed for a furry companion.

That night at dinner, she was still upset. She sat down at the table but refused to speak to her parents. She was tired of arguing and didn't want to cry in front of them.

Her parents tried only once to engage her in conversation before shrugging their shoulders and simply ignoring her. As her mother made last-minute preparations and began bringing food to the table, her anger began to build. She hated feeling that way and closed her eyes, attempting to steady her emotions.

Instead, she took two deep breaths, and then her eyes flew back open at the sound of her mother screaming in pain. The pot of mashed potatoes had somehow exploded right in her face as she carried it to the table. Her mother dropped what remained of the pot as she was struck with scalding hot potatoes and metal shards from the pot.

Rose sat there, stunned as her father jumped up to help her mother. She couldn't hear a word her father said as her mother's screams faded away. She just felt guilt and shame. Since that incident, she worked harder to control her emotions. She never had any fits of anger or any further incidents after that.

****

Jade was out getting her hair done when her moment arrived. She arrived early to her appointment and, after checking in, sat in the waiting room with a magazine. She could hear laughter coming from the two girls sitting across from her. She tried to ignore it, but the noise grew louder and louder as if trying to get her attention.

When Jade finally looked up from the article she was reading, the two girls averted their gaze. Nearly falling off their chairs, they laughed even harder.

As Jade rolled her eyes, her name was called. Breathing a sigh of relief, she walked past the two girls and sat in a chair. The stylist had just finished trimming the back of her hair when one of the girls took the seat next to her.

Jade fumed as the girl stared at her through the mirror with a taunting expression on her face. The stylist moved to work on Jade's bangs, and she was glad for the obstructed view. She had no desire to see the little girl any longer.

Then the laughter resumed. Jade bit her lip, trying not to let it bother her. But she could feel the anger boiling inside of her. She sniffed the air, smelling something odd. Just then, screams erupted from the chair next to her. Jade whipped her head around to see the commotion, almost getting cut in the eye in the process.

Her mouth fell open at the sight of the girl with her hair on fire. The straightener that was being used on her now lay on the floor, melted and mangled. *There's no way I caused that,* thought Jade. She shook her head, knowing damn well she couldn't control things like that. *But it'd be awesome if I could.*

That thought stayed with her for weeks after her appointment, and she noticed that similar things would happen when someone pissed her off enough. Something bad would always happen, even if she didn't directly wish for it to happen. That was enough for her to believe.

****

Lana's love of magic began sooner, having discovered an inkling of ability a couple of years prior when she noticed she could move objects with her mind. They never moved very far, but they still moved. She also learned that she could make things explode or catch fire when her emotions were strong. Lana kept her abilities a secret, but she still practiced them whenever she could, although she could never bring herself to cast a full spell from the book or intentionally harm someone.

****

"Okay, girls," Lana said as she stopped on a page about a third of the way through the book. "I think this is the one. This is the spell that will help us out with Veronica." As Rose joined her and bent over the book to check out the spell, Lana turned her gaze and asked, "Jade, did you manage to get a lock of her hair?"

Jade rummaged around in her bag. "I did, and it was a disgusting job. Please don't make me do anything like that ever again." She held up a plastic bag containing Veronica's hair. "She left her brush lying around in the locker room after gym the other day – made it all too easy for me. Here, take this." She handed the bag to Lana, who set it down next to a large candle.

"Hopefully, this is all we'll need."

"You're not sure?" asked Rose, looking up from the pages she was reading.

Lana shifted uncomfortably. "Well, I've never actually attempted anything like this before," she admitted. "But neither have the two of you."

"True."

Jade clapped her hands and rubbed them together. "So, let's get this started. I'm ready."

The girls gathered around the candle, and Lana placed the book in the center so they all could read it. Placing their left hands on the shoulder of the person next to them, they connected their circle. They each held a piece of Veronica's hair in their free hand.

They began to chant, softly at first. As they continued, their voices grew louder, and the pace quickened.

"Place the hair in the fire," Lana instructed. As they did, Lana closed her eyes, repeating Veronica's name over and over and chanting something in a language neither Rose nor Jade knew.

They threw each other a quick glance but remained silent, letting Lana finish. As she spoke, the room began to fill with a light fog, the flames dancing wildly on all the candles in the room. They cast eerie shadows all around.

As Lana uttered the last syllable, her eyes flew open; at once, the flames stopped their dance, and the fog disappeared.

"Whoa," said Rose in a near-whisper.

"Yeah," Jade added. "You think it worked?"

Lana closed the book. "Well, we'll have to wait until Monday to find out, but I've got a good feeling about it." She smiled, hugging the book close to her chest.

Chapter Three

The girls arrived at school extra early on Monday, eager to find out if their spell had worked.

"Jade, will you stop moving around and fidgeting so much?" Lana asked.

Jade never sat still when she was nervous. She was all over the place, pacing back and forth as her anxiety grew. Rose was the same way, except when she was excited rather than nervous.

They all looked as Veronica pulled into a parking space and hopped out. She greeted her friends, and then they walked right up to the front of the building.

"You freaks really should be kept hidden behind the school. You make the rest of us look bad." She laughed as she walked into the school.

"Not even a scratch on her. She still has perfect hair, teeth, and body…" Jade said in a mocking tone. "What happened?"

Lana shook her head as she grabbed her backpack. "I'm not sure. I guess it didn't work."

"Well, that sucks," Rose added.

"Sure does," Jade replied. "It's not fair. Nothing bad ever happens to her."

They continued to sulk as nothing happened until about halfway through the school day. The girls were in English class when their teacher suddenly stopped writing on the blackboard and fainted, hitting her head on the sharp corner of her desk. The class panicked, and a few others screamed as someone ran to get the principal and nurse.

Jade, Lana, and Rose just looked at each other with terrified looks on their faces. Mrs. Cooper was a favorite teacher of theirs. She had always treated the three of them with respect.

As the students sat in their classes, the principal announced over the intercom that class was dismissed for the day. Mrs. Cooper had died.

Chapter Four

"God, I thought they'd never let us go," said Jade as the girls walked out the front doors of the school. Parents with worried looks on their faces crowded the front of the building, waiting to pick up their kids.

Lana pointed to a woman running through the crowd. "Hey, Rose," she said, bumping her friend on the shoulder. "Isn't that your mom?" It was strange to see her there. She never picked Rose up from school. Lana had always given her a ride.

Rose never got the chance to answer. Her mother quickly spotted her and ran faster, tackling her daughter in a hug. "You're all right!" she cried out, checking Rose over for any scrapes or bruises.

"Yeah, mom. I'm fine." Rose wiggled out of her mother's grasp, giving her friends looks of confusion.

"What a freak!" Veronica said, laughing as she walked by. Jade glared at her.

Rose's mother tugged on her arm. "Come on. We have to go… now."

Rose didn't know what was going on, but it sounded urgent. "Slow down, mom! I'm okay. You're starting to worry me."

Her mother turned and looked Rose straight in the face, eyes full of tears. "But your brother's not," she said tearfully. "I got another call right before I got the one from your school. It was his coach. He's had some sort of football accident. It's pretty bad. He's in the hospital."

The three girls looked at each other with terrified looks on their faces. Rose's brother, Tyler, was a huge football star – the best in the state. He always had scouts after him. He'd never had an accident or been injured while playing. This was bad. This was really bad.

Her face pale, Rose silently nodded and followed her mother to the car. They drove off to the hospital so fast that they nearly had an accident themselves.

"You don't think…" Jade whispered, afraid to finish the sentence.

Lana shook her head slowly. "Of course not. There's no way we could have possibly caused all this." She didn't sound too confident in Jade's opinion, but she hoped that she was right. "Besides, we directed the…" she lowered her voice, glancing around to make sure that no one was listening in on their conversation, "... spell at the Veronica. If anything were to happen as a result of what we did, she should be the one affected – the only one. But look." She pointed to their enemy, who was laughing obnoxiously, tossing her long blond hair over her shoulder and flirting with every guy that moved.

"I know," Jade huffed. "Nothing happened to her… not even something as small as tripping in the hallway." She let out a small laugh. "I would have loved to see that."

"I would have too, but focus," Lana said sternly.

"Sorry."

Lana waved off her apology. "We have to figure out what's happening, and fast."

Jade nodded. "Agreed."

"So, what do you say we sneak out tonight and read over the spell we used. We'll see if we can figure out where everything went wrong."

"No," said Jade, shaking her head. "I don't want to go home right now. What if something terrible happened at my

house? I couldn't face it, especially if we were the cause."
She wrapped her arms tightly around herself.

"All right," said Lana. "We can go now. Come on."
She led her friend through the mess of people still standing
around outside of the school.

Veronica happened to be standing near Lana's car, so
they had no choice but to walk by her. "Where do you think
you're going, freaks?" asked Veronica. She sure loved to use
that word, especially when referring to them. "Don't you
think we all know that the three of you are responsible for
this mess? I mean, who else could it be?"

Jade opened her mouth to respond, but Lana pulled her
away and into the car. "we really don't want to start anything
right now," she whispered, trying her best to ignore the
laughter and accusing stares all around them.

Jade stared daggers at Veronica until they drove out of
sight, wishing she would just burst into flames or something.
"I really wish that spell had worked on her," she complained.
She sat back in her seat and folded her arms across her chest.

Lana chuckled. *Me too,* she thought. *Me too.* She drove
to the abandoned house as fast as she could, anxious to figure
out this whole mess. She could have sworn she did
everything right.

It would have been a huge help to have Rose with
them, but she understood why she wasn't. She had to be at
the hospital with her brother. He would need her.

When they arrived at the house, Lana parked in her
usual spot, hidden under a few bent tree branches. They
quickly unbuckled their seatbelts and took off towards the
front door.

"I'll check the Book of Shadows," said Lana, ducking to miss a low-hanging branch.

"Great, and I'll uh…"

"You can be in charge of the phones," Lana offered. "Maybe keep an eye out for any messages or any more emergencies."

Jade nodded. "Got it."

They hurried through the door, Lana tossing her phone to Jade as she went straight for the book. Even though no one dared to ever visit the house, she still preferred to keep it hidden. *You can never be too careful.*

Jade set the ringers on high volume to make sure she didn't miss any incoming calls or messages, then sat on the floor. She gently placed the phones in front of her and sat with her head in her hands, staring at the blank screens. She willed them to stay silent, not sure she could take any more bad news.

Lana located the book and quickly flipped to the page containing the spell they'd used. She read the whole thing over twice, thinking back to what happened when they cast it. She was sure they pronounced everything correctly and didn't miss anything or add any unnecessary words. She shook her head, frustrated and confused.

"I don't know!" she yelled, startling Jade. "I don't know what went wrong. I can't find anything."

"Maybe it wasn't us then," Jade offered, shrugging her shoulders. "We can't be the only witches in town."

Lana looked back down at the opened pages. When she had yelled out, she pushed the book away from her a bit, and it now lay at an angle. She squinted. There was some small writing she hadn't noticed before. Her hand flew to her mouth, and she slowly looked up to her friend, her eyes wide. "It was us," she said in a small, shaky voice.

Jade jumped to her feet, her heart racing. "How do you know?" she asked slowly, not sure if she wanted the answer, considering the dire expression on her friend's face.

Lana didn't answer. She simply pointed to the passage she'd just discovered.

Jade bent down to see what had Lana so worried. She located the words and read out loud.

"Beware this spell,
For it brings dark, not light
If unskilled in the art of magic,
You will invite
Death and destruction
Into your life."

"But what does this mean – that everything that's happening is our fault?" Jade asked.

Lana took the book from her. "I'm not entirely sure, but it sounds like it. It's definitely a warning that this spell is not what we thought it was – that it will do more harm than good."

Jade threw her hands up in the air. "So, what are you saying? That we just invited death into our world and that it's after us instead of merely playing a trick on Veronica?"

Lana looked up at her friend, overcome with fear. "Basically."

Chapter Five

"Oh, my god," Jade said, pacing back and forth. "What are we going to do? This is serious." She turned to Lana, who was still poring through the Book of Shadows, trying to find a solution – some way to reverse the spell they cast.

Spells can be reversed, right?

"I don't know," Lana answered, flipping furiously through the pages. "There has to be something, though. Something else we missed."

"Like what?!" Jade yelled, her voice echoing off the walls. "We already missed the warning. What more could there possibly be?" she asked sarcastically, though she desperately hoped there was an answer within those pages.

"As I said, I don't know," Lana replied, trying to keep her own voice calm. "But I'm going to find it."

"Well, hurry, please!"

Lana eyed her friend. She knew Jade didn't mean to be so bossy. She was stressed. They all were. She shook her head and went back to searching for the answer she was sure had to be hidden somewhere in the book.

Jade grew tired of pacing and took to wandering the rest of the house, leaving Lana to read in peace.

After what felt like hours of searching, Lana closed her eyes and rubbed them gently, giving them a break from the strain of staring at the pages. When she opened them again, she noticed that the room was filled with a cloud of thick, black smoke. She blinked a few times, thinking she was just seeing things in her exhausted state.

But the smoke remained.

"Jade?" she called out. "Jade, you're not smoking again, are you? Or knocking over any candles?" She didn't smoke all that often, but the last time she did Jade almost set the whole place on fire. It didn't help that the abandoned house was filled with leaves and twigs or that it was constructed from old, rotting wood. "Jade?" she called out a third time, with a little more urgency.

Still no answer.

Lana was starting to really worry. With each minute that passed, the smoke grew thicker, filling half the room. If there really was a fire, she needed to find Jade and get the hell out of there.

As she looked around, she noticed that the doorway was completely blocked by the smoke. It was the only way out of the room.

Crap. Lana sucked in a deep breath and, shielding her eyes with her arm, ran towards the door. Her skin began to burn whenever the smoke came into contact with her. She opened her mouth to scream, and the smoke quickly filled her lungs, burning the entire way down.

Lana began choking and fell to her knees, tears stinging her eyes. The air near the floor was mostly clear, but it hardly gave her any relief. Though the pain was excruciating, she was still determined to find her friend.

Clawing her way across the floor, she found herself at the bottom of the stairs. The last time she remembered seeing Jade was when she gave up her pacing and walked up the stairs to the second floor to wander around. Jade never could stay still when she was nervous or anxious.

Lana closed her eyes again and began to drag herself slowly up the stairs. Every inch of her body burned and strained, and her energy was draining… fast.

She kept pulling herself up until she ran into an obstacle. Eyes still closed due to the amount of smoke, she felt around with her hands to see if she could identify the object in her way. Whatever it was felt soft, yet heavy.

Prying her eyes open a sliver, she realized that the smoke was just too thick to see anything, so she quickly snapped them shut again. She had no choice but to try and crawl over it. As she began to pull herself over the obstacle in front of her, she stopped short when she felt something familiar… hair. Human hair.

Screams ripped from her raw, burned throat as she realized she had been trying to climb over the body of her best friend. Lana frantically felt around, trying to find a pulse or some other sign that she was still breathing.

Nothing.

She slumped back against the railing in defeat. She didn't know what to do. She didn't know where she was anymore, let alone how to get out of there. The smoke had scrambled her brain. Lana would have cried if she could, but her insides felt like ash.

"Lana! Jade! Where is everyone?" Rose cried out, coughing.

Lana had never been so glad to hear Rose's voice in her life. When she opened her mouth to call out to her friend, no sound came out. She then tried banging on the railing to get Rose's attention.

"Guys! Where are you? What is all this smoke? Is everyone all right?"

Her voice was getting louder, which was a good sign. It meant Rose was getting closer, and she would soon be rescued. Lana slid down the stairs towards Rose's voice.

"Oh, my god!" Rose screamed. "What the hell happened to you, Lana?" she asked as her friend tumbled down in front of her. Lana had been in the smoke so long that the skin on her face had nearly melted off.

Rose gagged. "Where is Jade?" she asked in a panicked voice.

Without saying a word, Lana pointed up the stairs.

Rose took off her sweater and covered her face with it, hoping to protect herself as she went off in search of her friend.

She didn't know that it wouldn't help. Nothing could. Once you spoke those words and unleashed the dark magic, nothing could help you. It wouldn't stop until you and everyone you ever loved was dead. The smoke, having done its job, cleared right up, leaving no trace of its existence.

No one ever managed to find those three best friends, as they remained a charred, molten mess of skin and bones at the bottom of the stairs in that abandoned house.

Let this be a warning to anyone wanting to dabble in dark magic. It is not kind; it will not do your bidding. If you mess with it, it will return the favor.

And it will not stop until it has snuffed out every last drop of light.

Made in the USA
Middletown, DE
18 January 2020

83172910R00102